Before I Was Me

Before I Was Me

Lisa Talbott

Lineage Independent Publishing
Marriottsville, MD

ISBN (paperback): 9781958418307
First Printed in the United States
Publisher: Lineage Independent Publishing,
Marriottsville, MD, USA

Maryland Sales and Use Tax Entity: Lineage Independent Publishing, Marriottsville, MD 21104

Contact: hurdmp@lineage-indypub.com
Website: https://lineage-indypub.com

*When the poppies shed their blood red blooms and float on a breath of air,
the blackened seeds rejuvenate, sprouting everywhere.*

*When the memories seem too painful for old soldiers who were there,
never speaking of the horrors to deaf ears that do not care.*

*That emblem now speaks volumes, a symbolic flower to wear, pollenating
nations; immortalized in prayer.*

Contents

Foreword

Lisa Talbott never ceases to amaze me with the depth and breadth of her writing. This book is no exception. From beginning to end, her ability to switch back and forth between… situations… (any more information would be a spoiler!) with precision and clarity makes "Before I Was Me" a riveting and engaging read.

My relationship with Lisa began not long after I established Lineage Independent Publishing in 2019. It was by chance that I stumbled across one of her poems (yes, she writes poetry, too!) on the social media page for a writers' group to which we both belonged at the time. It was a perfect chapter separator for my own third novel – so I reached out to Lisa and asked for permission to publish the poem as part of the book; she readily agreed.

Since then, we have co-authored a compilation of poetry and short stories and I have been the proud editor/publisher of all seven of her novels. The funny thing, though, is that Lisa and I have never met face-to-face: she resides in Portugal and I am in the United States. It is only through the wonders of the internet that we have been brought together in our endeavors.

Speaking of the internet bringing us together, since Lisa joined the Lineage Independent Publishing team, its stable has increased to include four other authors – three in England and one in Florida – who write in a wide range of genres. A simple search for 'Lineage Independent Publishing' on your retailer of choice's interface should give you the full list – which is now approaching thirty books, nearly all of which are available in paperback, e-reader, and virtually narrated audiobook formats.

Michael Paul Hurd
Author/Publisher
Lineage Independent Publishing
Marriottsville, MD, USA

1: Nine Years After

"Mum, where are my cycling shorts, the new ones I bought last week?"

Sarah was piling sheets and pillowcases into the washing machine. "I don't know Evan, think back to where you were when you last saw them," and Evan inwardly groaned at the same old 'lost car key' Lee Evans joke his mother used every single time he asked where anything was which would always have her chuckling away – but not her teenaged son, who had tired of hearing it ad nauseam over the years.

"I left them in the bag on the chair in my bedroom and the bag's not there now. You must've moved it," he said accusingly.

"Ah," she remembered, "I put it in your top drawer with your underwear."

He frowned and sighed loud enough for her to know he was miffed.

As per usual, Evan was running late for his cycling tournament, leaving everything to the last minute and expecting his mother to jump to his rescue.

He was fifteen now and had suddenly stopped talking about him being Eddie after the time they'd gone to lay a floral tribute on his grave, nine whole years ago.

Nine years ago! It didn't seem possible, but the evidence was before her very eyes. He looked so much like Miles – his father – that Sarah sometimes caught her breath.

It was his sixth cycling tournament and he'd won the last three, getting faster and faster, gaining a keen and admiring following. He had a more expensive bike each year as he grew, albeit adamantly keeping the British Racing Green colour. He ardently refused to consider a blue, yellow, or red. "Too fancy" he claimed, "I'm a sportsman, not a clown."

As the washing machine was loaded and started its cycle, Sarah reflected on how far he'd come since the day he was given his first pushbike for his third birthday and smiled remembering how he'd studied it cautiously, tenderly stroking the leather seat, spinning the pedals and asking his grandad to pick him up so he could sit on it.

She used to watch the recordings they'd made, often. The nights when Evan would be sitting in bed listening to stories and then start telling his own about when he was here 'before'.

How she wished to go back to those early days and learn so much more but was eternally grateful for everything she had managed to find out about her family lineage. They'd done their best, she and Bill, she acquiesced, but it had all been new to them, though with everything she'd learned subsequently, she knew they could have garnered a lot, lot more. Hindsight... that old humbug.

Evan had Eddie's medals mounted and framed which hung in his bedroom - all of them. His cycling medals, his war medals, his Tour de France photos, a whole collage of his past life that Bill had had professionally done before making the hard decision to move to Wales semi-permanently.

"Good luck, Evan," she shouted after him as he darted out of the back door, dressed in his new black cycling shorts and white vest.

"Yeah, Mum, same as that."

2: In the Beginning

Evan was that divine, perfect baby that rarely cried, slept through the night, lifted his body up on his forearms at only two weeks old and Sarah couldn't have been happier. Being a mum, albeit a single mum, was turning out to be the best thing ever. She was going to be both mother and father to her baby. She had her fabulous dad, who promised to be the best grandad her baby could ever wish for and so far, he'd been exactly that.

She couldn't wait to see what the future would bring. She was ready to embrace motherhood, in fact she had little choice because she was a mother now! Watching him sleep in his basketwork crib, she felt an overwhelming gush of love, and was sad that her mother wasn't here to enjoy it with her, with them all.

* * * * *

Two-year-old Evan:

"Mummy, before I was a baby in your tummy, did you know I used to ride a bike and win competitions?"

Sarah chuckled. She was always amazed at the things that came out of her son's mouth and his ability to string long sentences together even at his young age.

"Did you, sweetheart? Wow, I didn't know you could ride a bike."

"I can't yet, now. But I could before."

What did he mean, he can't yet, but he could before? Oh, Evan was a character for sure. He was like an old man living in a toddler's body. 'An old soul' as the saying goes.

Bill always used to say, "That boy's been here before, I tell you our Sarah, he's been here before."

And Sarah wondered if her dad was right and Evan had been here before, because she couldn't fathom how he always seemed to know things. But of course, that notion was preposterous. Reincarnation wasn't a given; it was purely that, a notion. Some believed in it, but it was never written down anywhere as being gospel. Besides, it was totally unimaginable that a dead person's soul could be reborn into another - especially that of her own son.

Sarah lived with Bill, her dad. It had been just the two of them for just over ten years since Pat was tragically killed in a car accident when Sarah was only nine years old. She'd been to the gym and was supposed to collect Sarah from school afterwards, but she never made it. Heart-attack, the coroner confirmed, after finding scarred tissue, and Bill accepted that as only a week prior to the accident she'd complained of horrendous chest pains.

It was a weekend as they were getting into bed and she declared "I had the most awful chest pains this afternoon".

Bill was concerned, naturally. "Honey, get yourself an appointment at the doctor's. You're not supposed to have chest pains for no reason. It might be nothing, but it won't hurt to get yourself checked. Do it tomorrow, OK?"

Pat smiled. Bless Bill for his unwavering compassion. "I will," she reassured him tenderly, never intending to at all!

Her car hit a tree where minutes previously there had been a group of school children waiting for the bus. Luckily, she missed those children, or that would have been even more catastrophic. Unluckily, because she'd ploughed into the tree that was waiting to be cut down by the council.

So young Sarah had been left waiting at the school gates for her mother to collect her. It was over an hour later before her dad arrived.

* * * * *

"My bike was silver and green and I was so fast, Mummy, much faster than Jack Kowalski."

Sarah took a sharp breath. Jack Kowalski? Where did he get that name from? She didn't know anybody with the name Jack, let alone Kowalski. And furthermore, how did he manage to pronounce the name?

"Jack Kowalski?" she enquired intrepidly as she poured herself a cup of tea at the breakfast table, noting he'd spoken in the past tense. "Is he someone you know, or knew?"

"Hmm" he nodded affirmatively, stuffing a spoonful of cornflakes into his mouth, "we're rivals."

Rivals??? Evan is two years old. He isn't supposed to know anything about rivalry.

"But I'm faster."

She joined him, nodding, then stopped because she felt it was too foolish to contemplate.

It was 7 a.m. and Bill would be descending to the kitchen imminently for his own breakfast before leaving to go to work. Sarah had two slices of bread in the toaster and the frying pan on the stove ready to make his fried egg.

"Grandad wants porridge today."

"Tough", she replied, "he's having his fried egg on toast. And how do you know what he wants anyway?"

Bill blundered into the kitchen with his snap bag, taking a large gulp of tea from his usual 'Best Husband' mug as Sarah pressed the button on the toaster.

"I rather fancied just porridge this morning, I'm running a little late." And Sarah looked to Evan and put out her tongue, conspiratorially.

3: 1867 – John Tyler, Windsor Castle

John Tyler had been dismissed from his service as a Coldstream Guard at Windsor Castle on health issues.

He'd been in the service since leaving school and was overjoyed at having been promoted to the very prestigious opportunity to stand sentry at Queen Victoria's bedroom. A privilege he never abused or underestimated.

Tyler was good looking too, if one was to see underneath that huge bearskin of a head covering! He was also an exceptionally loyal sentry. Whatever went beyond his vision or hearing in the Queen's quarters, would remain there.

John Tyler had never been brought up to gossip. It was ungentlemanly to do so. Oh, there were those that would have, and did, but not John.

He never forgot the first day she appeared on the balcony and spoke to him. He wasn't supposed to look or talk, but she insisted. "John," she said, "it is your name, is it not? Turn around and talk to me, goddamn you…"

Any monarch demanding you to turn around and speak to them is not an instruction to be ignored.

"… and take off that ridiculous hat for a moment."

John Tyler dutifully removed his busby, holding it under his arm as he stood rigidly, waiting to hear his Queen continue. He was nervous, and rightfully so. He didn't want to upset Her Majesty…

Queen Victoria pulled up a chair and sat on it. And then she did something that absolutely blew his mind: she placed a burgundy velvet pouch on her lap and pulled out a pack of playing cards and a handful of coins.

"Join me, will you, John?"

John Tyler was somewhat aghast: he was expected to sit down and play a game of cards with the Queen of England.

4: Evan (Present Day)

"Dad, there's a letter here for you, with an Australian postage stamp on. Looks like it's from Uncle Bob. Hope it's not bad news, Dad."

Bill took the envelope from Sarah and recognised his brother's heavy style of writing. "It is from our Bob," he said, opening it, and after a few minutes of reading, his face lit up. "Well, I'll be blowed. It's not bad news at all, Love. They're coming over for a visit… hang on… in June. Well, at least they've had the sense to come when the weather should be a little decent for them. Oh, how lovely, haven't seen our Bob since your mother's funeral. And they'll get to meet our young-un, too. Hey, Evan, what about that, then? You're going to get to meet your Great-Uncle Bob, my big brother."

"The one with the poorly foot that walks funny?" Evan asked.

"What?!? How the Dickens did you know about that, Evan?"

Sarah looked confused too. "What's wrong with his foot, Dad?"

"It was back in… ooh, what year would it have been? When was the Falklands War? Around 1982, I think. He lost his foot. Well, he caught a bullet, and it was so bad he had to have it amputated. Got a false one fitted. He actually caught a couple of bullets and it was touch and go at one time, but he pulled through OK, just lost his foot. But how did you know, Evan?"

Sarah and Bill looked at Evan waiting for him to answer. "I saw him, but he wasn't allowed to stay."

The toddler said no more as he continued to play with his building bricks on the floor, leaving his mum and his grandfather totally bewildered.

Sarah was still confused, mulling over what Evan had just said. "I didn't know all that about Uncle Bob. How come you never said anything?"

"Long before your time, Love. Bob was in the forces, you see. He's a fair few years older than me. Last time he was over here in Blighty was at your mother's funeral. Sylvia wasn't with him because she couldn't leave the children, and he stayed with his in-laws so you wouldn't have met him. Oh, just a minute… you did meet him, but perhaps you would have been too young to remember his limp, or even notice it."

Sarah nodded, of course she didn't remember him. "Why did he write a letter? Auntie Sylvia usually sends an email."

"Our Bob? Send an email? He leaves all that technical malarkey to Sylv."

5: John Tyler

After John left the Coldstream Guards and returned to Civvy Street, he and Annie moved to Southwark.

Their wedding had been low key, even though they'd been married in the chapel at The Tower of London, with Annie's sister as the only witness.

It was extremely rare for weddings to take place at The Tower of London, but John had built up a rapport with Queen Victoria and they'd often have nighttime chats. He'd confided in Her Majesty that he'd met and fallen in love with Annie Maynard and planned to ask her to marry him.

"And who is this spinster that has taken your fancy, John?"

John smiled at the Queen's description of his sweetheart. "Her name is Annie Maynard, Your Majesty. Her family came to England with the Huguenots. Her parents are French and I regret that they do not approve of our... erm, friendship."

"And why ever not?" she asked indignantly. "Have you disgraced yourself?"

John was appalled. "Indeed I have not, Your Majesty. I am an honorable man, but I am led to believe the family consider me unworthy of her hand. She is above my status."

Queen Victoria pondered his words for a few minutes. "Stuff and nonsense, how ridiculous. Well, John, give me the woman's details and I'll see what I can do."

He didn't know what she meant by "I'll see what I can do" until weeks later when she told him she'd approved for them to be married at the chapel in The Tower of London.

"This is not something I would allow on a regular basis, you understand, John. As you know, commoners are not permitted such a privilege, but I understand your intended is not just a mere commoner - such as yourself - so if you've truly decided to propose to this woman, I will have someone make the necessary arrangements. This will be my way of approval. And John," she almost forgot to mention, "white is my preferred colour for a bride to wear. Please make sure your woman wears a white gown."

And so the marriage took place on New Year's Eve. As a result, Annie was subsequently disowned by most of her family and two years later John was looking for alternative employment.

Eddie was their first born. Eddie loved bicycles.

6: Sarah

Sarah adored her dad, and they were very close. Bill struggled hopelessly for a long time after Pat's accident. He still had to provide for his daughter, pay the mortgage, the bills, do the shopping, cooking, laundry, maintenance on the house.

He was a miner working for the last open-cast mine in Leicestershire and had to leave the house early in the mornings, which necessitated him having to get Sarah up and ready for school at the same time. He had the good fortune of having the most understanding and accommodating next door neighbour with a daughter the same age as his own, and she would pop round to collect Sarah, give her breakfast, and take the pair of them to school.

This went on until Sarah was adamant she was old enough to manage on her own. She'd matured quickly, and even though Bill was reluctant for her to become a latchkey kid, he knew he could trust her. Besides, he had no alternative.

And they'd mackled along together just fine and dandy. Having to tell her dear dad she was pregnant was something she dreaded! She'd let him down; he was going to be disappointed in her and rightly so because although Bill had liked the lad - felt somewhat sorry for him - Miles had acute myeloid leukemia and was having regular blood transfusions. Bill was - as any anxious parent would be - concerned that his daughter wasn't prepared for what he could see to be the inevitable.

Miles had never tried to conceal his illness; indeed, he'd been very open about it, and Bill could totally understand their hurry to cram as much happiness into their lives as they could, while they could. And so, when Miles passed away, with Sarah - six months pregnant - at his bedside holding his hand, along with his parents, Bill was her tower of strength yet again.

How could he have been anything but thrilled to know his little family was going to be bigger and he was going to be a grandfather? He was only sad that Pat wasn't around to have had the opportunity of being a grandmother.

Sarah had a rough time during her pregnancy; she was having to deal with her grief and her wayward hormones. Her labour lasted for almost twenty-four hours and even then, the baby still needed help being delivered.

A midwife at the hospital asked Bill if he would like to sit with her and encourage her, suggesting his presence might be reassuring and give her some moral support, but he declined. "You'd have another patient on your hands if I were to be in there, Nurse. Thank you, but I'll just sit here and read my newspaper until the little lad decides to grace us with his presence."

The midwife smiled. "She's having a boy, then?"

"No idea, Miss. She wants it to be a surprise. Whatever it is, he or she, it's gonna be loved. Mark my words, he'll have three very doting grandparents."

Evan was Miles' middle name. Sarah had already decided that if they had a boy, he was going to be Evan. She prayed they would have a son.

*   *   *   *   *

Sarah was wracking her brains trying to remember the first time she gave a thought to considering Evan being 'forward'. As a new mother she didn't know what was normal progression. It may have been the time he pushed himself up onto his arms and his head was looking from left to right. She wanted to call her dad to come and see but Bill was at work. Or was it when he smiled at her and touched her face? Her heart melted.

He was out of nappies at twelve months and already walking. He was weeing in a potty and making small sentences. She'd been to stay with a friend for a weekend and when her dad called to collect them, Evan - in Sarah's arms as she opened the door to let him in - declared "Oh Grandad, I have missed you."

How did he manage to say that, and how did he understand what 'missing someone' meant? He was a joy as well as being a never-ending source of wonder. Hence Bill's constant anecdote was "that boy's been here before, I tell you." One proud grandad.

The statement Evan recently declared, "Mummy, before I was a baby in your tummy, did you know I used to ride a bike and won competitions?" was mind blowing. He hadn't got a bike for one thing, and 'competition' was a huge word for any two-year-old to come out with.

He'd mentioned someone called Jack Kowalski and that they were rivals. There were no neighbours with the name of Kowalski. Sarah had never heard of the name Kowalski, yet Evan said it as a matter of total fact.

It was approaching Evan's third birthday. Sarah was excited because her dad's brother and sister-in-law were coming over from Australia, so there would be a little birthday party so she could show off her son. At her suggestion, maybe her dad would go up to the attic and get some of the old photograph albums and videos down so the brothers could reminisce. They'd been put up there a couple of years after Pat's accident and Bill couldn't bear to see them gathering dust under the TV.

She tried to remember her Uncle Bob but considering she was only nine years old and just lost her mother, she acquiesced she was excused for not doing.

With two weeks left until their arrival, Sarah was looking on her iPad for inspiration to make Evan a birthday cake. She was hoping for a nice sunny day so they could possibly sit outside in the garden. Their garden was always lovely and colourful, no matter the time of year.

Evan was having an afternoon nap, so she was blithely surfing the net for a suitable and easy birthday cake to make. She was no baker, but surely it wasn't that difficult to do? And she found one so simple even she couldn't fail to produce - a penguin! So easy, she considered. Just a bog-standard sponge cake with a bit of black paper for its wings, etc., marzipan for its beak, and "Hey, presto!"

She clicked on a few more images so she could ensure she was going to get it at least half right… and then she saw the name. 'Kowalski.' There were lots of images of penguins, and she laughed out loud: Evan must have seen the cartoon characters on the TV and remembered the name! Oh, what a huge relief engulfed her. He was a normal kid after all, and all this chitchat about a certain Jack Kowalski was nothing more than a child's wild imagination and a love of cartoon characters. Evan would have his Kowalski penguin, just like he wanted. She could not wait to tell her dad.

"Well, Sarah, Love, if you're happy to think along those lines, then I'm happy for you but I can't admit to sharing your optimism."

"But Dad," she tried, laughingly, "don't you see? He must have seen the cartoon on the telly and remembered the name. It's the obvious explanation. There must be a Jack-what's-his-name who rides a bike, and you know what a vivid imagination he has."

Bill stood up from the kitchen table to put his empty dinner plate in the bowl. "I do, love. I do. And I understand everything you're telling me, but I can't help wondering how he knew about my brother's foot. 'The one who walks funny,' he said. Never met our Bob, has he? How do you reckon he knew about that then, hey?"

Sarah couldn't provide an answer to that question because she didn't know, either. She shrugged, "I don't know, Dad.

Maybe he got some memories of mine when he was inside my womb? Do you reckon that could happen?"

"I'm sure it can" he answered a little too belligerently, for he didn't share that belief for a second. "Now then, what are we going to buy the chappie for his third birthday? I thought I'd like to get him a small bicycle."

7: Bob, Bill's Brother

War was something Bob never considered having to anticipate when he decided to join the army. To him, it was merely a means of escaping the rules inflicted upon him whilst living at home under his father's strict regime. It was a regular income for one thing, little outlet, and freedom!

Oh, how wrong can one be? He remembered the journey over there, and experiencing the cold, so damned cold. He envied those young comedians coming over just to entertain the troops. Boothby Graffoe was a name he couldn't forget. Some young good-looking comedian who could crack a few funnies and leave without the worry of being killed for doing a duty just because he's fortunate enough to not have to wear a uniform.

Boothby Graffoe. It was a place he remembered, a village somewhere in Lincolnshire he'd passed through. He'd been to Mablethorpe too, why wasn't there a comedian named Mabel Thorpe? Perhaps there was. There should be. It was funny enough.

"Ten weeks, that's what the history book will tell. Ten weeks my arse, it was a bloody lifetime!"

"I took a hit in the foot. Oh, not self-inflicted, I must add. Not like they did in previous wars to get out of the conflict. Heaven forbid I'd stoop that low, though I couldn't in all honesty blame them.

"It's the fear you experience. There's nothing like it. We can fear the dentist when we know we have to get a tooth pulled and that's bad enough, believe me. But the guttural fear I'm talking about is nothing like the fear of going to the dentist to get a tooth pulled. It's a fear of dying. Of being shot, killed. Or worse - being shot and wounded and left in agony.

"Many times I cursed my stupid young self for joining the forces, leaving my family thinking I was man enough to fight a war. It takes a brave man to go into a battle zone.

"I took two damn bullets. One in the ankle and another in my shoulder, right above my heart. Don't remember too much about it because the morphine obliterates a lot, thankfully.

"I do remember some things though… and it might seem really daft, so I don't normally tell a lot of folk, but I remember this kid talking to me. He was a cute kid, and he seemed to know me and for some reason I seemed to know him, too. He told me I couldn't stay there. I don't know where 'there' was but I was pissed at the kid because I wanted to stay there and who the hell was a kid to tell me I couldn't?

"Yeah … Well, it was a beautiful place I was at and the kid just sat looking at me like I was some kinda eejit that hadn't cottoned on to something. Like, he was the know-it-all and I wasn't. He reminded me of my younger brother. That's all I remember.

"When I woke up, I found that fool - Boothby Graffoe - sat next to my bed. He often came to the infirmary to cheer us miserable sods up. He was writing a letter to his girlfriend; Jennifer, I think her name was. He was telling her he was coming home in a few days' time, and I hated that bastard there and then. He'd been and done what he was paid to do and would leave unscathed from the Falklands War, in the physical sense anyway. I hope the git didn't leave unscathed mentally."

*   *   *   *   *

Bob and Sylvia arrived at Bill and Sarah's house. The taxi driver quickly got out of his driver's seat and hurriedly got their bags out, all five of them, dropping them off outside the front door. Bob paid him and gave a hefty tip.

It was a glorious sunny June day and Bob was helping Sylvia with the luggage when Bill bounded out his front door and practically leapt on his brother, enveloping him in an almost uncomfortable bearhug. "Bob…" he managed, a little tearfully, "Bob!"

Sarah stood watching the long-awaited reunion of the brothers, Evan standing with his arms around her legs, and she had a lump in her throat. Sylvia walked towards her smiling from ear to ear, and hugged her.

*   *   *   *   *

Evan took an instant liking to Sylvia and wouldn't leave her side. He insisted Sylvia put him to bed, read him a story, take him to the toilet, make his breakfast.

Sylvia would wake up in the morning finding Evan snuggled up fast asleep next to her. She hadn't even felt nor heard him come into their bed.

Secretly, she was smugly delighted that her grand-nephew had taken such a liking to her, rather than his own great-uncle. It was as if the child knew her.

"Well, our young Evan has certainly taken a shine to you, our Sylv. He's barely left your side." Bill was hoping his voice didn't betray his underlying tinge of jealously. His grandson had indeed become besotted with his brother's wife.

"And likewise, Bill, I adore your sweet grandson, I'm green with envy that you have such an adorable grandchild and Bob and I are still waiting. I think our two are more interested in feathering their nests rather than building any." Bill felt like she was trying to say something but said virtually nothing.

Sarah decided to chip in, hoping she wasn't going to be stepping out of line.

"Well, I can't really blame them, Auntie Sylvia. It's hard work being a mother. You lose a lot, freedom, a social life, but having said that we've gained a lot, too, haven't we, Dad?"

Bill nodded proudly, "Been a godsend, he has, Sylv, a godsend."

Evan liked that word, godsend. He smiled, turning it over in his mind. "That's right, Grandad, I am a godsend, he did send me," causing everyone to laugh out loud.

Bob and Sylvia were staying just a few days with Bill and Sarah before they took off for a trip up to Scotland. They'd done the rounds, making the obligatory visits to family and promising to return in time for Evan's birthday tea.

Sarah reminded her dad again about the photograph albums and videos he was supposed to get down from the attic. He'd been putting it off, procrastinating, because he knew only too well that the memories would come hurtling back.

The only picture he hadn't stored away was his framed wedding photograph that had always hung on his bedroom wall and to which he would always say "Goodnight, love" before he switched off the light.

Bill never even considered the thought of remarrying. He would have felt disloyal to Pat's memory. Besides, his daughter and grandson were enough for him. When his shift finished at the open cast mine, he hurried in the shower, eager to get home to find out how their day had been.

His work cronies must have been driven bonkers with Bill's never-ending tales that he shared with everyone, never considering that they might not be at all interested.

8: Young Jack Kowalski - Before

Jack Kowalski had been born to Josef and Antonia in Poland at the turn of the last century. The name Kowalski was as popular in Poland as Smith was in England, in fact it is the second most common name. It means 'blacksmith' and if you were a Kowalski, chances are your father - and almost definitely a grandfather - would be/have been a blacksmith, except Jack's father hadn't been a blacksmith; he was a farmer, one of only forty-five in his village.

Many Poles had been migrating to England from as early as the sixteenth century, but later - at the end of the Nineteenth Century - Josef and Antonia had decided their only chance of survival - or indeed any quality of life, was to join the masses now heading over to London after the failed uprising against the Russian Empire.

Josef couldn't hold firm any loyalty to his homeland afterwards, nor did he feel safe anymore as the Ukrainians were randomly arresting Poles and herding them off to places as far away as Siberia, but just before he managed to put his plans into action, he too was arrested by the Ukrainians, labelling him a traitor who claimed he was betraying his country, leaking secrets. It wasn't true, of course, and he had been devastated to learn it was a once 'so-called arbitrator' who'd committed the ultimate act of betrayal and lied about him.

His punishment was dealt out in the most heinous manner, as two brutes held onto him firmly, dragging one arm forward. All five fingers on his right hand were then forcibly sliced off in the sawmill where they'd made him work and whilst he bit his tongue in an endeavour not to scream out in agony to satisfy his gleeful torturers, it was an impossibility not to.

He was at least given a stay in the hospital but died shortly afterwards due to basic cleanliness of his grossly crude wounds being denied. Sepsis is probably the modern term used these days, but malnutrition and infection were certain contributory factors.

Food had been notoriously scarce and rationed pitifully, inhumanely so, and as he ignored the grumbling of his starving stomach, refusing to eat anything provided in the hope his family would visit soon, he began to squirrel it away, saving every single piece of stale bread, waiting and waiting.

The Commandant responsible for overseeing the medical unit gleefully restricted any family visitations though

Antonia and his sister Mary persisted daily. Then one day, totally unexpectedly, the Commandant - seemingly having a momentary lapse of inhumanity - relented, though only allowing Mary - his sister - to visit, but by then it was all far too late. It was winter and the snow had been cruel and deep, the journey arduous, and by the time she eventually arrived Josef had already gone. She took his bloodied, bandaged hand in hers and wept as she watched the maggots wriggling and writhing, reminding her of the ugliness of where they were.

"Why does it have to be this way?" she whispered. "What did we do wrong?"

A fellow comrade in the next bed, already living on borrowed time himself, uttered "He kept asking when you were all coming. He asked every day. He saved all his bread for you. It's there; look on the windowsill. I guess it's all yours now."

Josef Pavel Kowalski had been maliciously left a sheet of paper and pencil by his bedside so he could write his farewell message to his family. As he was right-handed and his fingers severed, he couldn't even leave them any final words – so he took the proffered pencil and paper and drew a simple heart, with his left.

The ultimate act of humiliation had been his meager coffin, which was so, so small. The nails hammered on the top and sides to secure it to the base penetrated his pathetic emaciated body. Even the wood for his coffin was rationed.

Hence, Antonia and Mary felt an even stronger determination to depart Poland, without him, joining the exodus of their countrymen, ultimately ending up in a little village called Melton Mowbray, in Leicestershire after many bleak and dismal months of enduring life in the smoky city of London.

There was no luxurious accommodation to be welcomed into, just ex-army-type barracks in the middle of what appeared to be woodlands, but that didn't bother the girls initially as they were amongst genuine fellow kinfolk at least, determined to create a new life.

However, it wasn't going to be a smooth transition. There was the continuing struggle to understand the language for starters, and the barracks held no amenities such as flushing toilets, furniture, or running water. They'd left all their worldly goods and their past in Poland and possessed only what they could manage to carry, and that included the child. A single bed was going to have to be enough for them. Jack would continue to sleep on a blanket, on the floor.

One of the first things the expatriates decided to introduce was running water into each hut. The outside communal pump was always busy, and some ladies commandeered it too selfishly on wash day and tempers would fester. They all had an inside copper to boil nappies and warm the place. Fuel was in abundance around and no one went cold during the winter months. They rarely went hungry either, as the woodlands provided bountifully with rabbits, pigeons, squirrels, and the odd deer!

9: Questions and Answers

Bill had eventually found the perfect little bike he wanted to buy for Evan. He'd frequented all the shopping centres, toy shops, trying to find one that wasn't plastic. He wanted a sturdy bike, preferably with stabilisers, that would last, not some plastic monstrosity that would surely break after a week or two, and he found just what he was looking for on eBay.

Bill wasn't one for internet, gadgets, etc., but he was running out of ideas and time until Sarah suggested he look on eBay for a vintage bike. He cursed himself for not thinking about eBay and then patted himself on the back for finding exactly what he was after. It was metal, it was green, it had stabilisers, it even had a bell, and at €45 it was perfect. It was from Holland but he didn't care about the additional courier cost: it was for his only grandson and he was going to thoroughly enjoy teaching him to ride his bike.

"Sarah, Love, look here. I think I might have found one. What do you reckon?"

Sarah looked at the posting and smiled up at her dad's anticipating face, "It's fabulous, Dad. He's going to absolutely love it, isn't he? But don't you think it's a little big for him? I don't know if his feet will reach those pedals."

Bill wasn't going to be dissuaded. "I think that seat can be lowered," he said effusively, "I'm going to message the seller to ask. So, what do you think? shall I go ahead and place a bid?"

Well, there was going to be nothing Sarah could add to change Bill's mind. He was like a kid himself where Evan was concerned, and why should she even try to damper his enthusiasm?

"I can't believe you're even asking my opinion, Dad, when you've already made up your mind. Bid! Buy it now. Can we get it here in time for his birthday?"

It did arrive before his birthday, and fortunately it was delivered just as Bill was parking up after returning home from work. He was so excited he gave the delivery driver a twenty pound note tip instead of the ten he intended to! He hurriedly placed it in the garage until he could open it when Evan was in bed. Evan was going to have a lovely third birthday. He was having a penguin birthday cake, a bike, and his family. Miles' parents were also coming over to celebrate his birthday.

"Mummy, what does 'woe betide you' mean?" Evan asked out of the blue.

Sarah laughed, "Woe betide you? Well, it means woe betide you. Woe betide you if you do that again," she said, making her voice deeper and, well, woe betiding. Evan still didn't understand.

"It means… It's a little warning, really. If you continue to do something wrong, you will have to suffer the consequences."

"What are 'consequences?'" he asked even more perturbed. These questions from an almost three-year-old were baffling Sarah, and where on earth had he heard the expression 'woe betide you'?

"Consequences are things that result from something we've done, or not done, in fact. For example, let's say you threw your banana skin on the kitchen floor and I slipped on it and hurt myself. That would be a consequence of something you'd done. And then I'd probably say, 'woe betide you if you do that again'. Do you see? Anyway, has someone said that to you?"

"But I never put my banana skins on the floor, you put them in the bin. I would never hurt you, Mummy."

"I know you wouldn't, Sweetheart, that's just an example so I can try to explain it to you. And I would never do anything to hurt you, either."

Evan smiled. "You're my favourite Mummy. I'm glad I chose you."

"And I'm glad you chose me too, but if I had to choose Evan, I'd choose you a million million times."

Evan's face contorted into a contemplative frown whilst thinking about his answer. "*You* can't choose, Mummy. Only *we* can, like you chose Grandma. You chose her to be your mummy."

Sarah loved that idea, that she chose her mother. "Your grandma would have adored you, Evan. If she'd still been alive, I doubt I would get a look-in where you're concerned. She was a good mum, and your grandad misses her no end."

"What does 'get a look-in' mean?" Evan asked.

Yet again surprised at his never-ending thirst for answers to his questions, Sarah tried explaining what she'd just said. She cleared her throat, "Well, a 'look in' means to be involved. Your grandmother loved babies and I know that she would have done everything for you that all doting grandmas do. She would have fed you and bathed you, taken you to the shops in your pushchair, bought you lots of cuddly toys and read you stories at nighttime. Everything that I do for you. So, I probably wouldn't have had that chance, I wouldn't have had much of a look in."

Evan was fixated on Sarah, taking in what he'd just learned. "But she did do that, Mummy, before I came back. She looked after me and said if I came down to you, she'd be able to see us all every day."

Sarah was nodding and smiling as if to reassure not only herself, but Evan too. "Evan, Sweetie, I don't really understand what you're telling me."

Evan sighed, as if showing an adult version of frustration. "Before, Mummy! When I used to be Eddie."

Sarah was gobsmacked. She tried to push Evan to talk some more but he'd decided to shut up, declaring he wanted to watch some DVDs. She didn't want to push too hard but was desperate to know more. She looked at the clock praying it was time for her dad to be home. It wasn't; there was another hour to go.

She needed to remember everything he was saying so she could discuss it with Bill.

She put a random disc in the DVD player for him and rushed to her iPad. "You haven't switched it on, Mummy!" he called out. She left her iPad to go and press play on the DVD player. "Scatterbrain!" he said.

'Scatterbrain'! How many times had her mother called her that? Sarah had never used that word in his presence. In fact, she'd hated her mother teasing her with the word. Twice she'd been called 'Scatterbrain' by Pat and twice she'd had something of a meltdown. She remembered both vividly.

*   *   *   *   *

"Sarah," her mother called from the bathroom, "get a move on or we're going to be late for school."

"I'm ready!" Sarah called from downstairs, "where's my lunch box?" Pat had left it on the sink unit, where she always did, every morning.

"It's on the sink unit!" Pat shouted as she came hurtling downstairs…"

"I am not a nit Mummy. Why did you call me that?"

Pat had laughed out loud, "I said 'it's on the sink unit', not 'it's on the sink, you nit'. Goodness Sarah, you can be a bit of a Scatterbrain at times. Here's your coat, get in the car quickly, we're gonna be late."

That first time was lodged in the memory bank but not forgotten. The second time stayed and was never going to go away. It can be the simplest wayward comment an exasperated parent flippantly says that children never forget and take it with them forever, waiting - possibly decades - to bring it up at the perfect opportunity to remind the said parent of their infallibility of perfection.

"Sarah, you've got odd socks on again. Look, Darling, this one is white and this other is cream. How can you not tell the difference? Go back upstairs and fetch the others, you're being somewhat of a Scatterbrain today."

She'd felt belittled and embarrassed. She only want to please her mum and dad, not disappoint them. Being classed as a Scatterbrain made her feel she'd done something wrong, stupid, naughty.

* * * * *

Evan had never been called that word, nor would he, as far as she was aware. *Where did he get that from?*

She opened up her iPad and logged in, taking a cursory glance over her shoulder to ensure her little boy was watching the television. She clicked on Google and typed in 'my child talks about him being before'.

She felt kinda foolish until her screen became flooded with hits:

'The ghost in my child.''

'My daughter lived before, but she says she used to be a boy.'

'My son is my grandpa, reincarnated.'

'My child constantly talks of a past life.'

'My grandson remembers being a sniper in the First World War.'

'My daughter says she met her brother in Heaven. She was born after I miscarried our son.'

Sarah sat back in her chair as she watched everything on her screen. She looked over again at Evan, wondering if her son, too, had memories of a past life. Yes, he was different, he'd always had the gift of the gab and knew how to charm everyone. She'd always felt lucky having such a charismatic, knowing child.

A flashback came to her. She'd gone to the hairdressers a week ago, for a trim. Just a quick trim, nothing life-changing. There was an elderly lady sitting in a seat having her hair done, she was reading an old magazine. Evan had walked up to her and said "Your hair looks lovely, Pearl. Ray will love it too."

The elderly lady had turned to Sarah and asked "Do you know me?" Sarah had never seen the lady before and apologised on Evan's behalf. That was the day he'd asked her what 'a cheeky rascal' meant.

10: Bob and Sylvia

Anyone going to Scotland to do the touristy bit will know you cannot pass Edinburgh without doing the obligatory visit to Princes Street and the Grass-market which are both steeped in ancient history. It is full of awe and fabulous buildings and breathtaking scenery the further up north one ventures.

Sylvia was adamant she wanted to do a trip to the Isle of Skye. She wanted to cross over on the ferry because she'd had this haunting song in her head for as long as she could remember: "Over the sea to Skye."

The first time she heard the song was when she was at primary school, she was around six years old. Music lessons consisted of a teacher playing the piano and teaching them songs, music, and having their own musical instrument to muster.

Sylvia was no singer nor musician but favoured the recorder as it seemed the easiest to learn, next to the cymbals. That song, "Over the Sea to Skye" was compelling to her. As their teacher tapped out the tune on the slightly out-of-tune piano, she experienced goosebumps on her arms. For some unexplained reason, she wanted to cry as the feeling of actually being there enveloped and consumed her - and she had no idea why.

"Loud the wind howls, loud the waves roar,

thunderclaps rend the air.

Baffled our foes, stand on the shore,

Follow, they will not dare."

That first time of hearing the tune, she continued humming it in her head all the way home, not understanding why someone would consider the sea would cross to the sky. It was all wrong, she kept telling herself as she gazed up into the clouds, her young mind acknowledging that they looked similar. The blue skies like the ocean, the white clouds the foamy waves, and yet it wasn't.

She tried to recreate the notes on her already-previously-owned recorder, the mouthpiece chewed from past students. Her mother came into her bedroom eventually, practically pulling her hair out at the screeching and wailing sounds her daughter was producing as she and Sylvia's dad were getting ready to watch The Fugitive on the television which - in those days - was only shown on Tuesday nights.

When Sylvia finally drifted off to sleep, she was on an ancient bloody battlefield, but she wasn't Sylvia the primary schoolgirl anymore… She was a man. She was a killer, too, she felt as she withdrew her sword from the body of a man in a fancy, embellished red coat. She quickly wiped the blood on her kilt, and looked around for her next victim.

"Many the lad, fought on that day

Well the claymore did wield;

When the night came, silently lay

Dead on Culloden's field."

Young Sylvia tossed and turned in her single bed, sweating and shaking as the screams of the wounded and dying penetrated her dream. She was panicking. Geordie, where was Geordie, her little brother? He was next to her, waving the flag when they ran forward. But she wasn't this man wearing a tartan kilt and a sprig of heather attached to a sporran, she was just Sylvia, playing her recorder.

"Though the waves leap, soft shall ye sleep,

Ocean's a royal bed.

Rocked in the deep, Flora will keep

Watch by your weary head."

"Geordie, where are ye? Geordie, I cannae see ye… GEORDIE!!!"

"Sweetheart, shhh, shhh now, it's OK, you've just been having a bad dream. Shush now and go back to sleep. Would you like a glass of warmed milk?"

Sylvia was drenched in sweat and refused a glass of milk. "Mum, my brother was killed and he didn't even kill anyone. I saw him but I couldn't manage to save him. Why did he have to die? And I killed someone, too, Mum. I stabbed him with my sword, but Geordie didn't 'cos he was only there as the flag bearer. Why did they kill my brother, Mum? Why did the English want us all dead? I want to see him. I've got to go back and see him."

Sylvia's mother had no words. Her daughter's night terrors were becoming more and more frequent. Usually, by the morning, she'd forgotten all about them and had no recollection, until one particular night and then all of the following years.

*   *   *   *   *

As they disembarked the ferry and took their first footsteps onto Skye, Sylvia inhaled deeply, smiling. She closed her eyes and tilted her head backwards, feeling an overwhelming moment of nostalgia and calm.

"I'm home," she whispered silently to Bob, who hadn't heard her because the gulls were screeching overhead as he busied himself gathering their luggage. She chuckled - again to herself - pausing a moment to try thinking back... to gather her wits and remember...

"Geordie! Geordie MacDonald!" she heard someone shout in the distance, startling her reverie, "Boss wants ye in his office, pronto. Best not keep him waiting, lad."

A shiver ran down Sylvia's spine. Why would the name Geordie MacDonald cause her to react? She didn't know any Geordie, but as the teenager sprinted past her to go to the office, she had a flashback of a young boy from ancient times, with red wavy hair proudly waving a flag.

She hadn't noticed any young people on the ferry crossing to Skye, but it was a short crossing and with so many tourists on board it was easy to not see everyone, but as he brushed by her she had a moment of *deja-vu* and felt instantaneously nauseous.

11: Evan's Birthday

Tomorrow was going to be Evan's third birthday! Bill was beyond excited with the bike he'd managed to source and buy. Sarah had added the finishing touches to the birthday cake, which looked more like a demented vicar than a penguin, but she'd done her best. Bob and Sylvia were returning from their Scotland trip in time for the celebrations, and Miles' parents were coming over to join in, too.

Sarah had checked the weather forecast and sighed with relief to see that the sun was going to show its face for at least an hour or two in the afternoon, which was going to be just enough time for Bill to show off his culinary expertise on the barbecue. She didn't care anymore after that; they could take it all indoors and concentrate on spoiling Evan.

The morning arrived at last, and Bill was like a child himself. He couldn't wait for Evan to see his birthday gift. He'd spent hours polishing the chrome work of the handlebars and wheels, buffing up the seat and pedals and touching up a few paint chips. Considering it was almost a vintage bike, it looked almost spit new! He was chuffed with himself. He'd also made a little cardboard plaque which he'd fixed to the handlebars. It said 'The Champ'.

On the kitchen table sat a handful of birthday cards. Sarah could recognise the writing of them all. There was one from Miles' godparents, two from her friends, one from the neighbour, and the last one from her mother's bridesmaid.

In truth, she wasn't entirely happy with her efforts at cake decorating but anticipated Evan being excited.

The summer patio furniture had been brought out from the garage, cleaned and adorned with balloons and ribbons. Bob and Sylvia and Miles' parents would be over soon, and Bill was contemplating waiting for their arrival before giving his gift to his grandson.

"What do you reckon, Love? Shall we give it to him now or wait for the others to get here?" he asked Sarah.

Sarah was busy preparing the salad and putting the chicken drumsticks on a tray ready to par-cook before putting on the barbecue. She was listening to her dad whilst all the time ticking off everything she needed to do. Candles!

"Dad, where are those candles I bought for the cake?"

"Haven't a clue, Sarah. How would I know? Well, what do you think? Now or later?"

"Now or later for what?"

"His bike! Do we give it him now or wait for the others?"

"Oh! Oh, sorry Dad, I'm just a bit rushed. I don't know. What do you think?"

"I'm asking *you*!"

Sarah stopped what she was doing. She could tell her dad had been waiting weeks for this moment and she burst into a fit of laughter.

"Who's the actual child here, Dad? Let's give it to him now, and I'll show him the cake when everyone gets here. That gives him another surprise later. Go and call Evan and get the damned bike!"

Evan - for practically the first time in his short three years - was quiet, and Bill was anxious. He looked at the bike in awe. He studied it in silence whilst Bill and Sarah exchanged cautious glances.

Evan touched the handlebars and stroked the seat, gently. He touched the pedals and spun them once, and then again.

"Evan?" Sarah broached tentatively. "Do you like it?"

"Grandad!" he exclaimed tearfully, rushing over to Bill and hugging his legs. "You remembered! You remembered. Thank you, Grandad! It's just my like old bike."

Bill sighed with relief. "Your old bike?" he queried humorously.

"I mean my very first bike. My racing bike had gears. Green and silver. This is green isn't it, Mummy? British Racing Green?"

Sarah nodded numbly. It actually was 'British Racing Green', a deep, dark olive green. It was impossible for him to have known that. Bill and Sarah only knew that fact because of how the sellers on eBay had described it.

"Lift me up, Grandad. Let me sit on it."

Sarah wanted to cry, but Bill was obliging and encouraging him. "Can your feet reach the pedals, Evan? Here, look. Put your foot just there. No, don't stand up. Sit on the seat. Put your hands here, on the handlebars, and – "

Evan interrupted and folded his arms in a stance of defiance. "Grandad! I do know how to ride a bike, you know!"

Within minutes, the stabilisers had to come off whilst Bill had to attach wooden blocks to the pedals to enable his little feet to reach… And then the boy was off!

It was absolutely uncanny! He was three-years-old and - granted a little wobbly at first - falling off a couple of times, but adamant at getting back on and cycling round the garden, laughing until his pink cheeks ached. Bill was running around at the side of him all the time, unable to comprehend how quickly he'd managed to learn!

He was quite out of breath by the time his brother and sister-in-law and Miles' parents arrived. "I don't know about my Pat having had a heart attack, but I think I'll be having one if I have to keep this up! Right then, folks, time to eat."

The barbecue was lovely and so was the birthday afternoon. Conversations flowed easily and Erica and Steve, Miles' mum and dad, thoroughly enjoyed meeting Bob and Sylvia, wanting to know all about their lives in Australia.

"We considered moving out there ourselves at one time, didn't we, Steve? An aunt of mine emigrated in the 70s as one of those £10 Poms. They all went over on a big cruise ship and settled eventually in Perth. I think a lot of the English did, back then. They have a wonderful life and their families have grown so big! I sometimes wonder if we had gone, would Miles have had a longer life? Better treatment? But then again if we had, we wouldn't have had our lovely grandson, would we?"

Sarah laid her hand lovingly on Erica's. "Well, we're glad you didn't because of the same reasons. Evan is so much like Miles sometimes, it's painful, and my only regret, Steve and Erica, is that Miles never got to meet Evan and Evan will never know what a fabulous man his dad was, but he's lucky when all's said and done, our boy has a very loving family. Anyway!" she declared enthusiastically, "it's time for the birthday boy to witness his mother's abysmal attempt at making his birthday cake. Evan! Come and help me with the cake and you get to blow the candles out."

It was a moment of disbelief. Sarah knew the cake wasn't the best birthday cake of the century, but she'd done her darned best! It was carried proudly to the outside table, the sun still determined to make the day memorable, the three candles lit and everyone started singing the obligatory "happy birthday to you, happy birthday to you…" but faded slowing at the end of the recital when noticing Evan's confusion.

"Evan," Sarah asked, "do you recognise him?" Evan shook his head. He didn't.

"It's Kowalski!" she tried to remind him, enthusiastically, "the penguin, Jack Kowalski the penguin. I made him into a cake for you. Do you like him?"

Evan's face turned in a second and was filled with absolute horror. "Mummy! That's not Jack. That's a snowman. That's not Jack, that's not Jack. I don't want my stupid birthday cake, you Scatterbrain, you Scatterbrain!"

"Evan! EVAN!"

It was an absolutely unimaginable catastrophe. What had happened to her sweet, adorable, well-behaved little boy? The adults witnessing the child's inexplicable behaviour associated it with simply being over-excited. The 'terrible twos' had taken longer to come forth and was manifesting into his third year. Everyone laughed it off, except Sarah. It was there again, the reference to her being a Scatterbrain, the term her mother used, which she hated.

She couldn't hide her anger and wanted to take him into the house and give him a proper ticking off, perhaps a good hiding as well! Send him to bed without any birthday cake, but of course... she couldn't, nor wouldn't. She felt so disappointed and sure this was going to be a birthday none of them would ever forget.

12: Mary Kowalski

There was talk amongst the settlers of a dance night in the village and many were contemplating going.

"You should go, Mary. You deserve to have some fun," Antonia urged.

Of course Mary wanted to go and experience some frivolity, an occasion to wash her hair, her body, and put on clean clothes, but…

"Go, Mary, please. I have to stay here with Jack, but you need to have a life of your own. Come back and tell me all about it, and here… use my lipstick. Josef used to tell me I tasted of strawberry junket when I wore this lipstick. Your brother would insist you go."

The Polish people were hesitant upon entering the brightly lit village hall with the unrecognizable music seeping into the darkness outside. It felt crude, yet invigorating, and as Mary dared to take a peep inside, she was shocked to see happy couples embracing on a small wooden dance-floor. They were laughing, having fun, moving to the music.

"Your first time here?"

The words were spoken in her native language, and she looked around to see who'd spoken them. He was grinning, very tall and handsome, and – very forward as he grabbed her by the hand and led her inside.

"I'm having a beer. What would you like to drink?" Mary didn't know what she wanted to drink; she'd never been in this type of environment or situation before.

He had dark hair, brown eyes, and dark eye lashes. She noticed his shirt collar, slightly frayed, but clean. She scanned her surroundings, feeling the vibration of the music from her toes to her chest. "I don't know," she admitted feebly, hoping he could hear her above the noise of the band.

Jochen laughed at her evident naivety. "Punch it is for you, then. Come."

She almost had to run to catch up with him. The trestle table in front of the stage where the band was set up was filled with bowls of punch, all set out on white linen table cloths. Her eyes opened wide in amazement at the huge bowls filled with fruit and liquid. She'd never seen an orange before, floating in the alcohol, and wondered what the rest of the night would bring.

"Don't eat the skin," he warned, "it's bitter. You're just supposed to suck on it. Same as this one here: it's a lemon.

Do you know what a lemon is?" Mary shook her head: she didn't, but it looked pretty.

"It's worse than the orange, but good in some drinks. What is your name?" Jochen asked.

Mary was overwhelmed and not at all accustomed to having the attention of a very confident, good-looking, man. It was her first legitimate night out since her arrival in the United Kingdom and she was totally out of her depth.

"Mary," she answered feebly, "I'm Mary Kowalski."

Jochen grinned like a Cheshire Cat, "Hello, Mary Kowalski. I'm Jochen. Jochen Rysz. Will you please dance with me, please?"

No matter what music was being played, Jochen and Mary never left the dance floor apart from a couple of times going to refill their glasses or to the toilet. Mary felt lightheaded at the end of the night, whether it be from the punch she'd consumed or the atmosphere. It was as though all the ugliness of the world had evaporated into a sense of purity, and she didn't want it to end. But when 11 o'clock arrived, the band stopped playing and the lights were switched on, leaving the room in full light. Mary laughed when she noticed the dance floor was devoid of other dancers and it was just her and Jochen.

"All good things come to an end, *Kochanie*," he said staring into her eyes, "I must see you again. Next week, yes? Promise me now."

Antonia was fast asleep. "Antonia, Antonia! Wake up, wake up, Antonia, please? I've had the best night of my entire life, I've met the most wonderful, handsome man. Antonia… I think I've fallen in love."

13: Evan

Evan was up at the crack of dawn the next morning, riding his new bicycle around the garden. He had this determined expression on his face, pedaling faster and faster.

Sylvia stood watching him whilst nursing her coffee cup, a tad hungover from the alcohol they'd all consumed after Evan had gone to bed. Erica had wanted to stay, to continue the celebrations until whatever o'clock it was, but Steve was driving and kinda insisted they left.

"I get him," she said to a confused Bill who had joined her at the kitchen window watching Evan riding his bike. "I get him, Bill, because it's true. He's right, you know. Your little grandson out there is goddamned right and a little miracle, but we're either all too stupid to know or too ignorant to admit it."

"Sylv? More coffee?" Bill offered.

She shook her head in annoyance at her brother-in-law's lack of acknowledgement and attempt to diffuse the conversation. "He's real, you know, Bill. I'm talking really real. You should listen to him. Take notes, record him, video him, whatever, but make sure you get it all down because if you don't, you'll regret it. They forget… after a while. Their memories dissolve like a snowball melting in the summer sun, and then it's all gone. All that remains is a wet patch. You remember what a wet patch is, don't you Bill?

" 'Course you do. You'd turn your back on it and wait for it to go away and Pat would eventually wash those sheets and you wouldn't have a clue nor give a damn… Just like you're doing now."

"Sylv! Hang on a minute, there's no need – "

"Oh, what, Bill? You know it, Sarah knows it. Come on, we all know it. Bob and I only have a couple more days before we fly back home and I, for one, would love to know his story. Wouldn't you?"

Bill pursed his lips together and nodded, not taking his eyes off Evan. "I've said it times, Sylvia. I don't know… There is just . . something about him, even when he was only days old. It was like he'd always been here. Do you know what I mean?"

"Out of the mouths of babes, you mean? He's still only a baby, but I'll bet you a dollar he will have a lot more to say as he gets older. They forget everything later, but sometimes something will happen to jog a distant memory. Ha, it happened to me, too."

"Sylv?" Bill was puzzled.

"Oh, I don't remember much now, Bill, but I'm pretty sure I was here before, too. That's why Bob and I went to Scotland. I've always had this yearning to visit the Isle of Skye, ever since I heard 'The Boat Song' when I was a child. And do you know that the second I stepped foot on the island, I felt I'd come home."

"Go on, Love," Bill urged.

Sylvia took a deep breath. "I'd never been anywhere remotely close to Scotland, ever, and had no Scottish connections that I know of, but I had these recurring dreams of being in a battle somewhere, yet I wasn't me in the dream, I was a man. I had a little brother, and he was killed in the battle – which didn't seem fair, he was just the flag bearer. I'd be screaming so loud that my mother would rush to my bedroom to see what was happening. She said I had night terrors. Well, I suppose if one dreams of being in such a frightening situation, one *would* scream.

"I wore a kilt, and I had a sword. It was heavy. My brother's name was Geordie, I think? Bill, I have a sister. I've never had a brother, so I cannot explain why I had those dreams or why I felt like I had to go to Skye, but dear Lord, the feeling when I got there… Like I say, I felt I was home."

69

Bill was silent, trying to digest what his sister-in-law had told him. "And our Bob, have you told him?"

Nodding, she answered "I have, yes. He's a bit on the fence, like you. Thinks it was all just a crazy mixed-up dream, and perhaps it was but I've never heard of anyone dreaming of themselves as a different sex or a different age! We didn't have the internet when I was a child, so my parents wouldn't have been able to do any research, unlike yourself. Didn't you say Evan mentioned a rival, someone called Jack Kowalski? I'm sure you might be able to find something if you looked."

Nodding towards Evan riding his bike in the garden, she continued, "He seemed pretty upset yesterday with his birthday cake, and Sarah seemed pretty upset when he called her a Scatterbrain."

"Yes, well… Yes, he was upset and the poor girl had gone to a lot of trouble over that damned cake. Can't imagine where he heard the word Scatterbrain 'cos it's not one either me or Sarah use. It was one Pat used from time to time and our Sarah didn't like it, but… Oh, I don't know Sylv. I mean, I've always said he's been here before, but it's just something folk say, isn't it?"

"Indeed, Bill. Indeed, folk do."

70

14: Antonia Kowalski

Although it was difficult living in the barracks, Antonia felt safe living amongst her own people, being able to communicate in her mother tongue, and of course she had her sister-in-law, Mary. She felt safe because these people had shared the same mindset to leave Poland.

There was a wonderful camaraderie and the children played together without too much falling out.

Jack was growing. She'd already been given many hand-me-downs which she'd altered to fit him – she was a fine seamstress – but she wasn't prepared to live in these conditions indefinitely.

Mary had been seeing her young man, Jochen, for months now and Antonia, whilst delighted for her happiness, would feel a pang of envy as she watched her sister-in-law excitedly ready herself to meet him. Mary missed Josef dreadfully but wouldn't entertain the idea of another man.

How she longed for a job she could go to, just for a few hours to give her a break and restore some dignity to her life. Earn some money to be able to indulge in something as simple as a new lipstick. The one she had was almost gone now. It was red, and had been Josef's favourite.

One evening, one of the men returned to the barracks telling of how he'd heard some Poles had been given accommodation by the local Council. Just a small one-bedroomed place but it had an inside toilet with a bath! It sounded luxurious to Atonia, too good to be true in fact, but she became desperate to know more.

Over the next few months, the population grew less at the barracks with many now being rehoused in Council-owned flats or prefabs. Antonia, Mary, and Jack were eventually given a two-bedroomed prefab house, just on the outskirts of the town centre. It was like a little palace, they gushed. It had a postage-stamp sized garden where Antonia hoped to grow a few vegetables. Mary had been fortunate enough to land a little part-time job in a jeweler's shop and everything seemed to be looking up.

One evening Mary returned home absolutely shattered. She'd carried a sewing machine back with her. A lady had come to the jewelers with various pieces of gold she wished to sell, after the death of her mother. The lady was clearing everything, she explained. Beds, furniture, a sewing machine, curtains, bed linen, pots and pans, the lot. Mary explained that she was only employed part-time and wasn't in a position to negotiate buying but when the owner returned, she would be certain to show him.

Her English was also much improved now, too, and dared to ask about the other items the lady was selling. After their discussions, Mary went ahead and purchased the sewing machine for Antonia, promising to have more items when she'd managed to save enough from her wages.

Antonia was worried. "Two shillings, Mary! That's a lot of money. We can't afford it. You must take it back and apologise for your recklessness. We can't indulge in non-essentials yet. We have food to buy, furniture to fill this house. What were you thinking?"

Mary was hurt. "Actually, Antonia, I was thinking maybe you could earn some money working from home. The hard times are practically over now and people are spending money again, buying new clothes – wedding dresses even – and drapes for their windows. You can do all that! The lady's mother was a valued customer at the jeweler's so she was given a good price for her things. She has other items she wishes to sell, too, and I've arranged with her to have more. She has beds, furniture, fabrics. Atonia, I don't feel I am wasting money. It's all used merchandise and we can't afford to buy new. She wants very little anyway; she says if she doesn't manage to sell everything, she will have no alternative but to give it all the Rag and Bone man. I believe the Rag and Bone man is a scrap dealer."

Antonia calmed down and looked at the machine in its polished wooden case as it sat on the floor. Indeed, a sewing machine would be a boon. No more hand-sewing Jack's trousers. She could make drapes for the windows; she could perhaps make herself a new skirt and blouse. And for Mary, too.

"Dear Mary, how selfless you are. Thank you so much. You're right, I can do that. This machine will help us no end. I'm sorry for my outburst. Thank you again."

Their living arrangements were working perfectly. They shared the chores, and they shared young Jack. When Antonia was working on her sewing machine, Mary would take Jack out for a walk. When Jack was napping, Antonia would take the opportunity to sew or tend to the vegetable patch. It was during one of these quiet moments that Mary dropped a bitter bombshell: she and Jochen were going to get married.

"Not for another few months yet, Antonia, but hopefully before December. Neither of us desire a winter wedding, and Jochen already has a house so you will have this place all to yourself once I'm Mrs. Rysz. Jack will be going to school soon, so you'll have lots of free time to concentrate on your sewing."

It was unimaginable that Jack would be starting school soon, where had the time gone? Of course Mary was going to get married and leave, that was natural, and Atonia wouldn't have wished it any other way, but she was going to miss her. She was going to miss their chats, their laughter, their friendship.

"And I'm going to buy a bicycle for Jack for his birthday. And don't give me that shock, horror look, because I've already put a deposit on it. My nephew deserves to be treated on his birthday after all, and if his favourite aunty can't do this one little thing for him, then give me a good reason why."

Antonia fell about laughing. Favourite aunty? He only had Mary.

Her wedding dress was simple, modest, and miraculously finished in time. It had been difficult to find buttons. None of the shops had any that were suitable, and Antonia then had the tedious task of making them all, which had taken days, but Mary looked exquisite in her satin bridal gown. Her long dark hair was scraped back into a tight bun at the top of her head and the short lace veil encircled around it.

"I'm nervous" she confided to her sister-in-law as she was fixing the 'something borrowed' necklace behind her, "were you, when you married Josef?"

"Of course I was, all brides are nervous. I'm sure all the grooms are nervous too, but you have a good man, Mary. You'll be very happy. Your parents would be very proud of you. Now hurry, let's go. We don't want Jochen to think you've changed your mind."

15: Evan

Months had now passed since Evan's birthday and the novelty of having a bike hadn't waned. Bill was still dithering about pressing him over the things he'd said, rethinking what Sylvia had advised him to.

He found it hard to accept that his grandson had been reincarnated because there was no solid proof of any such thing but at the same time, intriguing. He wasn't ultra-religious. He was a decent hard-working, honest chap and considered he must be relatively OK because the church roof hadn't caved in on the rare occasions he'd stepped inside one.

He wondered how it could be, this concept of reincarnation. He recalled Evan once saying, "everybody can come back." He couldn't recall any memory of a life before, and he doubted whether he would want to come back again.

"Does everyone get a second chance? Surely not. Why would God give a serial killer another shot of being alive because they deserve to rot in Hell. Did they rot in Hell? And if Heaven is so perfect, why would anyone want to leave?

Where was Pat, had she been reincarnated into another child?"

How could he find out?

Nothing made any sense to him, and he wished Sylvia was still here so he could discuss it with her a lot more. If Evan was someone else before, would he grow up to be that person again or would he be someone entirely different?

Oh, it was all far too complicated for Bill. "I'm a miner," he reminded himself. "I work at the open cast mine digging for coal. I'm a dad and a grandad and I haven't a clue, I guess that makes me clueless."

It was Saturday afternoon and Sarah had gone into town to meet up with some of her old school friends, leaving Evan with his grandad, who'd promised to take him to the park so he could have a long cycle ride once they got to the park.

Evan watched Bill carefully put his treasured bike onto the back seat, like it was a fragile article. "Up you get into your seat, Buddy, and I'll buckle you up."

It was the park in Hugglescote, next to the cemetery where Pat was buried. He felt guilty for not visiting her grave in a long time but it was painful, so he'd only go on her birthday, or Mother's Day. He knew she wouldn't mind.

"Life is for the living," she'd say, "not to waste valuable time tending old graves. Don't ever do that for me, Bill, 'cos I won't be doing that for you. Bury me in the back garden if it's allowed, but only if I die from natural causes. Don't want you getting any ideas of taking me out before my expiry date!"

What a shock that had been, what a horrible nasty shock. He was bewildered, angry, *very* angry, and lost. He was lost because their world had turned upside down and was never going to be the same again. Well of course it wasn't going to be the same again because now he had to be everything and he had a daughter to raise.

The grief was horrendous, and he had to force himself to function – for Sarah's sake. Sometimes he found himself praying to a God he wasn't sure existed, for someone to take Sarah away so that he could be allowed to grieve alone. Yes, his neighbours had been amazing and he was truly appreciative, but his strength left him on many occasions, and he despised himself often for wishing he didn't have a child to consider.

He thought back to Sarah after Miles had died. She never begrudged Evan's being, like he'd done, hers. He never once heard his daughter curse for being left alone with a baby, ever.

"Grandad, careful with my bike, please."

Bill laughed. He was always careful with the bike. "Here you go, Son. Mind the holes in the path! Off you go, I'll catch you up."

Evan had gone like a shot and Bill walked steadily behind him. The park was full of local kids, some even fishing in the brook. When he was a kid, that brook seemed enormous, and everyone would say the same. Jumping from side to side would be a challenge with many ending up in the cut and dreading going home to show their parents their sodden shoes.

One of his earliest memories was his brother coming home from the park one Sunday afternoon, disgraced.

David wanted to go to the toilet but there were no toilets at the park. He shouted to his friends that he needed to leave but they all ignored him. Nature took its toll and David ended up fouling himself and his cronies screeched with laughing, chanting "He's bobbed his pants, he's bobbed his pants. Bobby, Bobby, bobbed his pants."

Mud sticks, in more ways than one, and from that unfortunate mishap, Bill's brother David would forever be known as Bob. Bill doubted his brother would have ever revealed to his wife why he was Bob to everyone, rather than Dave.

Kids. They can be wonderful, but they can be so cruel. He watched Evan cycle round and round the park, ignoring the other kids enjoying themselves on the swings and slide. He didn't even seem to notice the other children there, or want to integrate with them, and yet Evan was extremely sociable.

"You want me to push you on one of the swings, Evan? Take a rest from cycling?"

"No, Grandad, I have to get fit."

Get fit? He's three-years old! "Why do you need to get fit?"

"For the race, Grandad! Jack's getting fit, too."

Jack! Again!

Bill knew he had to continue pushing, "Is Jack here then?" he asked, looking around for anyone else on a bicycle.

"Of course he isn't. Jack doesn't live here; he lives in Melton. I need to get fitter, faster."

Melton! He'd named somewhere. He would store this in his memory bank and write notes when he got home.

"Erm, well… How old *is* Jack?"

"Grandad! You Scatterbrain, you know how old Jack is, same as me!"

Bill cringed. He'd said Scatterbrain again! And then Evan said something that blew his mind into fragments: "Go and see Grandma Pat and me before. I need to practice alone."

"Practice." "Go and see Grandma Pat and me before."? It wasn't real. It couldn't possibly be real.

Bill couldn't answer because he was totally bewildered.

16: Eddie Tyler

John and Annie Tyler eventually left Southwark, London, and moved to a little village in Leicestershire, Ibstock. They purchased a shop on the High Street where they both wanted to put the past behind them and build a life for them and their now expanding family.

Eddie was a good son; he was well-behaved with an enormous sense of humor. Many siblings followed, including his brother Johnny who he could only vaguely remember as Johnny died as a toddler and he was too young to understand. May was next, then Meg, then Rose, but he wasn't interested in any of them really, apart from Meg. He liked to tease her, as an older brother is wont to do, and Meg could never be allowed to retaliate because her mother would always side with her first born.

The shop on the High Street was paid for in cash after John's departure from the Guards. His apparent dismissal through ill health was never diagnosed or talked about. He went on to become an engineer whilst Annie and their daughters managed the shop.

Eddie had developed his cycling proficiency and became somewhat of an enigma in not only their little village, but the surrounding ones, too. He was now a teenager and had won many cycling races. His parents swelled with pride and displayed his trophies in the shop. He could do no wrong.

He customised his own bicycle, spray-painted it British Racing Green, but keeping the handlebars sparkling. He polished the leather seat with dubbin oil and scraped every scrap of debris from the pedals with an old toothbrush. He tended to that bike like it was an ardent lover.

"See this, Meg," he once said while she was heavily engaged using the mangle to squeeze the water out of the sheets on washday, "this is what true love is. A means to find yourself. It represents freedom. Do you wanna take a ride with me, on my bike? You've never done that, have you? Come with me, Mum won't notice."

So she did. Oh, she knew there was going to be Hell to pay when she got back for not completing the laundry chore, but an adventure with her big brother was not to be missed. She experienced the thrill of the wind in her face as she sat croggy in front of her brother, tucking her dress between her legs.

He cycled quickly down the High Street, turning left at the Church and freewheeling until he needed to start peddling again before they reached Overton Road when he told her to open her eyes and feel the freedom as they experienced the exhilarating speeds Meg never imagined in a millions years. They splayed their legs as they sped through the 'water splash' that crossed the path and laughed heartily as the cows in the adjacent field raised their heads at the disturbance of peace.

That ride out with her brother was something she would never forget and totally justified the scalding she received for neglecting her housework chores. Eddie hadn't been reprimanded for taking her away, but he did at least help her to finish her chores.

It was possibly around 1910 or 1911 when they made their very first batch of ice-cream and Meg had been instructed to walk around the village selling it in a push-along barrel. Ice-cream was considered not only a rarity but a luxury!

There would be no thanks to Meg for her efforts, indeed it was considered her due. She was mortified some time later when her mother declared at the dinner table, "I've found a job for you, Meg. It's in Manchester. You're going to have to go into service. You'll be having to leave soon."

Everybody bowed their heads in silence. Meg felt she was being punished for something she couldn't comprehend. She looked over to Eddie who refused to meet her gaze. She looked beseechingly to her father, her mother…

Meg was the middle daughter. May was older and Rose the youngest. Why her?

"Eddie, please speak with them. I don't want to go away. I won't know anybody in Manchester. Why are they sending me into service when I'm needed here, in the shop? Help me please!"

Eddie was flippant with his reply. "Our parents must have discussed what's best for you, Meg. They're obviously seeing the bigger picture for you. I'm sure this must have been a hard decision to make. They know your worth here."

Meg couldn't agree. "Then why me and not May? She's older. Or Rose, who's younger? It's OK for you, Eddie. *You're* number one. Are you going to help me or not?"

Eddie shrugged, looking at his wristwatch. He had another competition in two hours' time and didn't need the stress.

"When I get back, I'll talk with them, OK? But Meg, think of it. Manchester! A brand new opportunity with a regular income all for yourself. You'll meet different people.

It will be amazing. And you'll have holidays, so you'll be coming back."

Meg was bitterly disappointed with her brother's lack of empathy towards her impending expelling from the family.

Eddie was now dressed in his competition attire and hesitantly stood back watching as Meg continued turning the handle of the mangle for yet another laundry chore. "A kiss for luck for your favourite brother?" he begged.

Meg never turned to look at him, "Same as that."

Eddie raised his arms wide in submission, not understanding. "The same as what?"

She was determined not to face him, because she was still angry. She turned the mangle faster. "Don't come crying to me for sympathy, either."

17: Sylvia

Sylvia and Bob were back in Perth, Australia, and it felt good to be back home. The heat was a welcome change to the so-called British summer, confirming all their decisions to emigrate.

She filled the kettle to make a cup of tea then turned it off after hearing it heat up for a few seconds. It was 6.30 in the evening and if it wasn't the perfect time for a gin and tonic, then when was?

Bob had taken the suitcases out of the car and hauled them into the dining room. "Where shall I put this lot?" he asked like a child asking a teacher an equally stupid question.

She wanted to be daring and tell him exactly what he should do with them because she was tired, exhausted after the long flight from London to Perth.

Bob knew the luggage wasn't going to remain in the dining room. Any idiotic husband knew that, but for some reason he needed his wife to tell him what to do with them. However, Sylvia was feeling somewhat brave.

"Surprise me," she replied flippantly, handing him a glass. Bob looked confused as he took the proffered glass.

As they drifted back into their routine life, Sylvia was consumed with thoughts of their trip. The Isle of Skye, Evan. She hoped Bill would heed her advice and record everything, do some research like she wished her own mother had done. Oh, hindsight is a wonderful thought. Why did she only know so little?

She decided she might try doing a bit of research herself. She felt an affinity with the Isle of Skye and had a vague feeling she might have had a brother named Geordie. She didn't know why she thought that, but when she heard someone shout the name as they were disembarking the ferry, a shiver went down her spine.

Even to do this very day, Sylvia would hum the Boat Song. *"Carry the lad that's born to be King, over the sea to Skye."* But as far as she was aware, there had never been any battles on the island.

Bob had planned a Sunday afternoon golfing with a couple of his buddies and that was just dandy for her because she would have hours to herself to do a little internet digging.

She started off researching the Boat Song but became very confused because the original version differed from the latter, and if the version she knew was contradictory to the original, why had she dreamt she was in a battlefield? She

continued reading and came to the conclusion that perhaps…
and that was a big 'perhaps'… she may have been a Jacobite
and fought in the battle of Culloden? Then why the
connection with Skye? Surely none of the Skye Crofters
would have travelled all the way to Inverness!

It wasn't making sense to her, so on a whim she decided
to look to check if any battles had actually taken place on
Skye. And surprisingly she found something extremely
interesting.

She stared blankly at the screen on her iPad and felt the
familiar shiver all over her body. It was right there in front
of her. The MacDonalds clans against the MacLeods from
all the neighboring Hebridean islands – over five hundred
years ago! Lewis, Harris, Skye, Dunvedon, Sleat. It was an
utter bloodbath.

Eventually she sat back in her chair and closed her eyes,
trying to picture the scene and again she had this strange
feeling. MacDonald? She knew no one of that surname, yet
it felt 'familiar'. She knew that in her dreams she'd been a
man but had no idea as to whom she may have been - IF she
had been there, of course.

She was now regretting not doing this internet search before their trip to the UK because then she would have been much better prepared. Now she had to rely on her iPad.

She started to make notes, listing dates, names, etc., she was going to record as much as she could.

18: Eddie

Eddie cycled up the side entrance of the shop and put his bike in the shed. He was exhausted but ecstatic: he'd won the race and had another trophy for his mother to show off to all her customers.

He was home just in time for dinner, and everyone sat around in an usual quietness, waiting for him to announce his good news. He entered the dining room grinning like a Cheshire Cat.

"Here you go, Mother. Another for your collection," Eddie beamed.

Annie and John arose from the table and hugged him, congratulatory. The others followed, each bestowing their congratulations, except for Meg.

Eddie looked over to her, "Nothing from you, sweet Meg? Don't I get a little peck on the cheek, even?"

She was still smoldering from their earlier talk, but everyone was watching and waiting for her to make a move. She rose likewise, and hugged him, "I had no doubt," she whispered, "you were always going to be number one."

Eddie took his seat at the table and poured himself a glass of water while his family watched. "Kowalski was too close for comfort today. He was second, but I tell you, Dad, he's been working hard. I can't lose sight at this stage because he's flying. No, Mum, not too many potatoes, I can't afford to put on weight. Jack's like a whippet! But it's all good fun."

The meal was eaten with the normal quietness, no elbows on the table, no more chitchat.

"Eddie," his father said after the plates were taken away, "I have some grave news for you."

Eddie gave a half-hearted chuckle. He was on a high and doubted anything could dampen his spirit.

"War has been declared, Eddie." John shook his head at hearing the words leave his lips, "You're going to be called up."

Everyone stared in utter shock. "Dad!" "What?" It was unbelievable that a war could be happening.

"Eddie, Son. Please don't enlist before you get your call-up papers. Your mother and I are begging you."

Eddie gave another disbelieving chuckle, then focused on Meg. "Looks like we're both going away then, Meg," and he picked up his glass of water to 'Cheers!' her.

John and Annie were devastated and couldn't hide their feelings. Eddie was their first born, their pride and joy. The others came along as a matter of progression, but Eddie was... well... he was their everything.

Annie couldn't sleep. She would conjure scenarios to keep him at home. Maim him in some way, lock him up in the attic, poison him enough to make him unfit to go, deprive him of the opportunity to fight for his country.

"What mother wouldn't go to such lengths?" she asked herself. How many other mothers had lost sleep worrying about their sons going into battle? Who made the decisions? Men, most definitely. Women would never have allowed their babies to kill or be killed.

May was supposed to be going to be married to Will, but no doubt those plans would be put on hold because Will would be going to war too. Meg would still go to Manchester, so Annie would at least have her out of the way. Rose was still young; she could cope with just Rose.

It was July, 1914. Eddie Tyler stood proud in his uniform, excited to be participating yet disappointed at not being able to compete in the Midlands Cycling race - which of course was cancelled until further notice.

His two sisters hugged him and wished him good luck. His parents sobbed on his shoulder, and he felt a tightening in his throat. He looked around for Meg but she wasn't there, so he hurried back in the house, ran upstairs and knocked on her bedroom door then walked straight in.

"Not coming to wish me good luck then?"

Meg was lying on her bed writing in her journal. She closed it and stood up, giving her brother the once over, touching his shoulder and appraising his uniform.

She smiled at him, "You don't need me to wish you good luck because you are going to be one of the lucky ones, Edward Tyler. You'll come back. You'll see."

"And how do you know? Nobody knows."

Meg laughed. "How many years have you known me, Eddie? All my life, of course, yet you don't really know me, do you? Let me tell you why I didn't need to come downstairs with the others to wish you good luck: because I *know* you will come back home safe and sound. I know that, and I also know that you will meet my future husband, Albert Knifton. He will be a sniper somewhere in France and you will befriend him. I'll marry Albert but it won't be a happy marriage. You won't, either."

Eddie was speechless, for once. He didn't know how to reply to her because, yes, he did know that Meg had these weird thoughts but the whole family would dismiss her ramblings. France? Is that where he was going? What was she talking about? What did she mean 'you won't, either'?

"I'm going, Meg. Please, wish me luck."

"Same as that," she replied.

19: France, 1914

Eddie:

Eddie was horrified to find himself in filth. He stunk because he'd not bathed in ages. His feet hurt because his toenails had worn out his socks and rubbed on his boots and he had nothing with which to cut them. They were given a little water to shave but he felt it was sacrilege to use when it would be better used for drinking.

The trenches were waterlogged, muddy, cold, dismal. He watched the others scribbling on bits of paper in their moments of aloneness. Eddie didn't have a pencil, nor paper. He wished he did have. He used to always have a pencil and paper handy…

The firing had started again. "Knifton!" he heard someone shout. "Look over to see who you can pick out!"

"My head's just as important to me as yours is to you, sir. *You* look out!"

Eddie laughed, admiring the man's bravado, as indeed it was. And then he remembered his sister's last words to him. "You'll meet my future husband, Albert Knifton."

Eddie sat up then, "Hey Knifton, what's your name. Your first name, I mean?"

"Bert," he replied, "why would you ask? It doesn't matter what our names are. We're just names and numbers going to be forgotten eventually, like the rest of us that are forced to fight for something we don't give a shit about."

"Albert Knifton?" Eddie couldn't stop laughing. "Albert Bloody Knifton!!!"

"Laugh at me again soldier boy and this bayonet will rip your insides out. Friend or foe, neither my blade nor bullet has a conscience on this killing field."

"Bert, I'm not laughing at you, honestly, but I feel I do have to tell you to chill out a little cos I've been assured that you and I are gonna survive this war and you're going to marry my sister. Hmm, might not be a happy-ever-after cos she told me it wasn't a match made in Heaven, but it can't be worse than this, hey?"

Bert was not amused, "Sir!" he shouted loudly, "I'm going over the top, as ordered. I think I'm just about prepared to die, sir!"

Albert Knifton:

"So, erm… what's she like then, this sister of yours?"

Eddie was massaging his toes and his ankles. He'd taken off his rotting socks and was dreading having to put them back on, though the odour of his decaying feet was nothing compared to the stench of the trenches they sat in.

"Meg? Ah, she's knowing, Bert. She's always been that way. Some say 'she's been here before', know what I mean?"

Bert nodded like he was supposed to understand but hadn't a clue what he meant.

Eddie continued and leaned back into the wall whilst he enlightened Albert about his future wife. "My sister has this knack of just knowing stuff, even before it's happened. Get this, Bert... she says we're all related to King Alfred. You know, that guy that was supposed to have been shot in the eye with an arrow? Meg's adamant we are and she knows. I don't know what makes her think these things but I'm telling you, she's never wrong. I think if she'd been born a couple o'hundred years earlier, she'd have been burnt at the stake."

Albert looked at him in confusion. "And how has that been proved?"

"Oh, yeah, of course we can't prove that, but I'm talking about other stuff... There was a pianist came to play in our village, months ago. All the family went, except Meg. I talked to her, tried to encourage her to join us but she was still sulking with our parents for arranging for her to go to Manchester. And then she said something real strange, she said 'He's going to regret coming here'. I asked her what she meant, but she just shrugged and said 'you'll see'. And she did tell me I'd meet you!"

"And you could be making this all up, like your demented sister. Nice try, but bugger off, Tyler."

Eddie laughed because he actually believed in his sister and though his war years were truly horrendous, he felt confident he'd be OK.

* * * * *

"We need someone to make a drop-off and the only method of transport we have is a bloody dysfunctional bicycle which will take days to get there," Colonel Rogers belted out.

"It's our only chance, sir." Eddie replied.

"It's NO chance, you fool. It's like sending the proverbial lamb to the slaughter. No! I'll not allow it."

Colonel Rogers paced slowly back and forth for a moment, then conferred with his aide in hushed tones. He then turned back to Eddie.

"OK, congratulations, Tyler. After due consideration, you have been specifically chosen to shine. I've been duly informed you're somewhat of a cyclist, is that so?"

Eddie saluted proudly, "Four counties champion and many more accolades to come after this damned war, sir!"

Colonel Rogers was saddened to hear that. His own grandson was aiming for the same. Would he have sent his own grandson under the same unforgiving circumstances? Definitely not.

"You're to meet with another cyclist soldier, his name's Kowalski. He's been ordered to meet with you at – "

Eddie's face lit up as he interrupted, "Jack Kowalski, sir?" He continued grinning, "Is it Jack?"

Colonel Rogers squinted, not sure how to answer, and just shrugged.

Eddie threw his head back and laughed out loud. "Then consider it already done before you have time to shave in the morning. We're rivals, sir, of old. Please tell me, does he know it will be me?"

"But the bike, it's not – "

"I can fix it," Eddie interrupted again, "whatever needs fixing. This is going to be a walk in the park for me, sir.

Thank you for the opportunity. Now then, please show me my orders."

Colonel Rogers went over the plan with Eddie. "Twenty miles away there's a burnt out farmhouse, just here," he said pointing at the map. "Fella that lived there... sorry... lives there, is in hiding. Built himself a cellar years ago, we don't ask why, but he's there, he and several other Frenchies who despise the enemy. Pascal. That's all we know, perhaps not his real name but who cares? Anyway, Pascal and his cronies have been, erm... assisting us for a while."

Eddie wasn't 100% convinced. "How do you know this Pascal fellow is legit? What if he's batting for both sides? I could be walking into a mine field. And how has he been assisting and to what purpose? And what am I going there for?"

"Yours is not to question why, yours is just to do or die, Tyler. Your task is to meet with Kowalski and do the drop-offs. You will park up your bicycle when you arrive at the ruin and pretend to be mending the tyre. Kowalski will be watching. He has his own instructions."

It was all so very vague. "I see," he said sarcastically, "it's just the same as you telling Knifton to look over the top and risk getting his head being blasted off, and you're basically telling me to do the same thing. Jack, too. We're just disposable fodder I guess, Colonel Rogers?"

Colonel Rogers was ashamed. "We *all* are, unfortunately, soldier. Dismissed."

Eddie fixed the bike as best he could, under extenuating circumstances. At least it had a chain, wheels, handlebars. No tyres, they'd long deteriorated; no seat either, which wasn't a problem as Eddie upended a boot from a dead soldier onto the metalwork. Makeshift tyres were concocted from the hides of dead horses, cut into thin strips and wound round and round the chrome work.

He was actually looking forward to his liaison with Jack and wondered if Jack knew he was meeting with him. He felt sure he would do. They would have this blissful escape to reconnect and talk about their cycling proficiencies, slap each other on the back, embrace perhaps, and continue their years-long teasing as to who was the best, the fastest, the fittest.

Their reunion was nothing as exciting and pleasurable as he anticipated during his task as Eddie was horrified to see his rival looking so different. Jack was gaunt. Likewise, Jack was equally horrified to see his rival looking so emaciated.

It wasn't all the smiles and hugs either had anticipated; it was a moment of realisation.

Eddie spoke first. "Jack, we both have a job to do but we're ahead of schedule. Let's sit and talk. We owe each other a few minutes, yes?"

Jack nodded and set his bike next to the hedge alongside Eddie's. They both sat down, looking across at the ruin and scanning their surroundings cautiously.

"Cigarette?" Eddie asked. Jack took one from the proffered packet, lit both his and Eddie's and inhaled deeply.

"Never had you down as a smoker."

"I never did until I came to this hellhole. You look great, by the way." Eddie lied.

"Yeah? You too." Jack lied.

"Jack, what's the deal? I've been told diddly-squat. I'm to meet you and that's it."

Jack looked over to the ruin again, nervously. "They'll be watching us, Ed. We can't stay here too long. I have to get back. You, too. Was your bike totally horrendous?"

"Look at it man. It's worse than that, but hey, it got me seeing my old friend again."

Jack then cautiously took out a package he'd had concealed under his coat. "This is what I have to leave under one of the bushes. You have to leave yours too. Ed, I don't know any more than you. Good luck, my friend, and goodbye."

Eddie stood up and went to mount his bicycle, and as he started to ride away, he turned slowly and waved. Jack waved back; "See you when we go home, mate. Can't wait to pass you at the finishing post."

Eddie gave him the middle finger, laughing as he pedaled the route he'd just cycled, "In your dreams, Kowalski, in your wildest dreams."

20: Evan Goes to Nursery School

"Dad, can you believe Evan is actually going to start nursery school tomorrow? We're going to wake up one morning and find ourselves packing him off to college or university!"

Bill was reading the Sunday papers and folded it upon hearing Sarah's profound statement. Time flies, that's for sure. Bill screwed up his face, digesting her words and remembered Pat saying the very same thing about Sarah going to school.

"Hon," Pat said, *"can you believe our baby starts school next week? Where has the time gone? "*

It had flown, the time. It always does. Months, years, centuries. Or is it relative - time? Does it even actually exist?

There are no past lives - according to those with alternative opinions and beliefs - because those thinkers declare there is no past. There is no separate human soul, either. The idea of self - based on alleged learned concepts - some consider illusory. Just as reincarnation is a misconception based on the teachings of the Buddha that was designed to show that you (the real you) are all things at all times. Everything is an expression of the one true self.

*Only existing in this very moment. The past never happened,
it's just a memory, or a form of learning and growth. Hard
to digest, but we'll never know... or will we?*

Evan was going to nursery school - was embarking on a
new chapter of his life. It surely wasn't five minutes since he
sat waiting anxiously for him to emerge into his world. Bill
was a grandad now and his very own baby girl, a mother!
Where indeed does time go?

"Dad, did you hear what I just said? Evan starts nursery
school in the morning. Are you going to take a rest day and
come with us?" Bill nodded perfunctorily, of course he was
going to have to, but he'd forgotten to mention it at the office
when he clocked out on Friday. It was no big deal; he'd sort
it out in Tuesday. His grandson's first day at nursery wasn't
to be missed.

"Is anything worrying you, Dad? You seem a little
preoccupied."

"Am I? Oh, I'm sorry, Love. No, no. Everything's
dandy."

"Dad!"

"What? No, Sarah, really. It's just that... Well, your
Auntie Sylvia keeps sending me messages. About our lad,

you know. About the things he says and him being forward, and the like. She reckons the same thing happened to her when she was a youngster."

"What exactly, Dad? What same thing happened to Aunt Sylvia that's happening or happened to Evan? Everybody dreams, whether you remember them or not, that's a proven fact. I love my dreams; I can't wait to sleep to experience them. Do you know that one of my most recurring dreams is that I'm in a house somewhere. It's not our house, here, I don't know the house at all, but it's beautiful and I'm finding the most amazing rooms full of gorgeous things."

Bill listened and watched as Sarah described the dreams he'd never heard her talk of before.

"Sometimes I'm with Mum. She's opening doors to show me what's inside the rooms, which are majestic. Some are really dilapidated and need a lot of TLC but I kinda acknowledge that the place could be truly awesome. Dreams are so bizarre; do you know Dad, I once dreamt there was a little girl sitting on my bed, talking to me. She told me her name was Sarah, and I said she couldn't be Sarah, because that was my name. She was adamant she was Sarah and got quite upset with me for disbelieving her. It's funny, cos I can remember that dream as if it was last night."

Bill didn't comment because he was speechless. He'd almost forgotten!

"It's just like that, Dad. Dreams play on our minds. And yes, I know Evan did say something about Uncle Bob's limp and talks about some Jack Kowalski character, and being a cycling champion, but you and I are down-to-earth enough to know it's impossible that's he been reincarnated, as you're seemingly hell bent on suggesting!"

Bill walked away to retrieve his phone and tapped in his code to open up his messages from Sylvia. He showed the screen to Sarah.

"Forgive your old dad for being something of a numpty then, Love, but here's something to think about. Have a read about Jack Kowalski."

*   *   *   *   *

Evan was uncharacteristically subdued as he was walked into his nursery school class, holding on to his grandad's hand with his right whilst clutching his new lunchbox, with his left.

The children already there rushed over to greet him enthusiastically and Mrs Evans knelt before him, with a big welcoming smile. Evan felt surrounded, and uncomfortable.

"I'm Mrs. Evans and you're Evan! We have similar names, see. All these children here felt just as nervous on their first day, as you must do. But don't worry, sweetheart, you will have fun here. We do lots of nice things, like painting, playing, building. Let me show your mummy where to put your lunchbox and then you can get to meet everyone else."

Evan spotted a boy on a small plastic tricycle and giggled. "Mummy, look," he whispered to Sarah, "it's not even a real one, is it?"

Bill and Sarah felt bereft leaving the nursery with Evan inside, and drove back in relative silence, until they approached the cemetery and Bill noticed the gates open. He slowed down, wondering whether to suggest they take a stroll to visit Pat's grave. They had no flowers to place, just their presence. "Shall we, Sarah? Shall we go and talk to your mother?"

Sarah had never visited her mother's grave. She didn't invest in the whole concept of "wasting time mourning a tiny plot of land with a slab of marble on top." She would have preferred a cremation, but Bill couldn't do that. It seemed too final.

"Dad," she sighed mournfully, shaking her head, "she's not – "

"I know what you're going to say, Sarah, but please come with me. I want to go. Please." It was more of a demand than a request.

As they walked the path together, each engaged in their own thoughts, Bill said "He told me to come and see Grandma Pat, and him before... When I brought him to the park. I didn't know what he meant, *him before.*"

"Dad –"

"I know what you're going to say, I know. I don't know, but what if he was meaning to tell me to visit your mum's grave and his grave, as he was in the past? What if he's trying to tell us much more than we can possibly understand?"

Sarah didn't reply immediately. "So you're suggesting we try looking for Jack Kowalski's grave or Evan's grave? Are you trying to say my baby is already dead and he's buried somewhere here?"

Bill was shocked at her loud retort. "He never said *he* was Jack Kowalski, Sarah, and I never suggested anything like what you've just said, but perhaps Evan is doing. What if the Evan before, is buried here?"

They both collected Evan from nursery, eager to hear his stories of his first day. They met with Mrs. Evans to ask how things had gone and were surprised when she asked if Evan had a sister. "No!" Sarah laughed, "I can assure you Evan is an only child."

And Mrs Evans, in all seriousness said "But he asked me to call Meg, his sister, to come and collect him. He was pretty upset, and kept saying over and over, '*Meg will know what to do. Please tell her to come. Tell her it's Eddie.*'"

"And I asked him again, I said, 'You mean Evan?' but he kept telling me, no. He told me he was Eddie. Is Evan adopted?"

Bill glanced at Sarah and Sarah deliberately avoided his gaze, still smarting from earlier.

"Mrs. Evans," she proclaimed softly and politely, "I have the stretch marks and the stitches down below to know that Evan is most definitely my son and he has no siblings. I'm sure today must have been a little overwhelming for him. He'll settle down, given time."

Things were becoming more and more weird.

21: Eddie and Albert, Back in France, 1914

Eddie arrived back at the trenches, none the wiser about his mission.

"What's it like, out there, I mean?" Bert asked.

"Well," Eddie began, "France is nothing like my mother spoke of. Though I don't know how she could have described it so ardently seeing as she never lived here. I suppose the memories were handed down to her."

"Your mother's a frog then?"

Eddie sniggered, "And I'm the ugly toad waiting to be kissed by the beautiful princess waiting to be turned into a dashing prince. Her ancestors are French, they all fled during the French Revolution, along with the Huguenots. Long time ago, Bert, but we still receive parcels from an aunt, occasionally. Silk stockings and lace. That kind of thing. Oh, and a little sailor's suit for my little brother, Johnny. Poor sod only got to wear it for his funeral. My parents moved to Ibstock after my father left the Coldstream Guards. They have a shop on the High Street now and – "

Bert perked up as he interrupted, "You're from Ibstock?"

"I am," Eddie answered, quizzically.

"Well, blow me down! I'm from Coalville. Standard Hill. I took you for a Londoner with that fancy accent."

"I was born in London and both my parents are Londoners so I suppose it's natural that I take barths and drink out of glarsses. Standard Hill! Blimey, Bert, do you know how many times I've free-wheeled down Standard Hill? Hundreds!"

The pair were laughing so much upon realising they were practically neighbours.

"That sister of yours didn't know that then, did she? Probably not such a 'Mystic Meg' as you like to proclaim. And anyway, you never did finish telling me the story of the pianist who was allegedly going to regret his visit to your village. What happened?"

"Damn and blast if I can remember his name, Bert, but yeah, anyway, on their way home they were involved in a car accident. His wife died and he ended up in a wheelchair. 'Mystic Meg,' hey? I like that. Got any spare paper, Bert? I think I'd like to write home now. I think I need to tell my 'skin and blister' I've met her future husband. God help her."

The two guys became friends and often joined each other during the rare moments of silence from the barrage of gunfire and blood-curdling screams. Often they wouldn't feel the need to talk; it was simply a comfort to sit and say nothing.

"Do you ever count them, Bert?"

Bert looked at him in horror, and disgust. "Count them? What kinda stupid question is that? Unlike you with your racing, I don't get a trophy every time for my skill. I'm ordered to pick them out randomly, no matter what they're doing. I'm the one that makes widows out of young brides that pray every night for God to keep their husbands safe. I'm the one that causes a mother's heart to break when the dreaded postboy delivers the telegram to inform her that her precious son was killed in action. Action? Do you know the worst thing, 'oh privileged one that gets to escape this Hell from time to time', was when I was ordered to shoot a man while he was taking a crap. He was taking a crap, for Christ's sake, just like we all do, but he wasn't even allowed the dignity to do his ablutions…"

Albert choked on his words, "I refused, but Rogers put his gun to my head and promised to use it if I disobeyed an order. So… it was either him or me."

Eddie felt terrible, and ashamed at his idiotic question. "I'm sorry Bert, I wasn't thinking."

Bert nodded, he couldn't possibly know how many, he didn't want to know how many. Far too many!

"When we meet our maker on Judgement Day, what do we tell Him, hey? Are our actions justified because we were just following orders? Are we going to be forgiven, given a heavenly medal and all our earthly sins forgotten? Our slates wiped clean? I don't think so, Tyler. I have leave coming up soon… I think I'd rather face the firing squad myself than come back to this…"

Eddie looked at him in shock, "Bert! Please don't tell me you're thinking of doing anything stupid."

Bert didn't answer him. He'd been contemplating for days. The thought of a week's leave was bliss. The thought of returning was torturous.

Their silence was interrupted by a huge blast, followed by the same screams they'd almost become oblivious to.

"Patterson! Blythe! Hudson! Knifton! Hurd! Congratulations, men, you're all going back to Blighty for a short vacation. Don't forget to send us a postcard and leave nothing to our imagination. Tyler, your cycling skills are needed again. Come."

Eddie looked over to Bert who was almost grinning; he had that look of relief on his face. He was afraid, considering their last conversation. Eddie had to follow Colonel Rogers but desperately tried to make eye contact with Bert to urge him not to follow through on his thoughts, and return.

He never thought him a coward; on the contrary, Bert was one of the bravest men he'd ever met.

Eddie's orders were for another rendezvous with Kowalski, which pleased him. It was again another opportunity to meet up with Jack and an escape from the stench and death of the trenches.

"Bert, will you take these letters to my family, please? There's one for my parents and one for my sister, if you have time, of course, I don't want you to go out of your way. You can meet her, Meg. You'll like her, everyone does. And then come back and tell me all about our hometown, tell me if that old scoundrel Cheney, the shop on the corner of Standard Hill, is still selling bootlegged whiskey. Ask him to fill your hip-flask. It's the least he can do for the war effort, seeing as though he managed to 'accidentally' get his and his brother's feet damaged."

Albert smirked, he'd heard the gossip about Cheney and his alleged brother and couldn't blame them. They were much safer at home than being amongst men who felt too macho to want to understand. Every village needed a corner shop where they could go to buy fresh vegetables and meat procured locally. Folk had become complacent about turning a blind eye but never enough not to heartlessly post white feathers through letterboxes, anonymously.

22: Evan, Age 4

Four-year old Evan loved bath-times. Sarah and Bill shared the task before putting him to bed and reading him a story. He preferred his grandad to read the stories as Bill would play-act according to which story he was reading, whereas Sarah tended to rush along, eager to get back downstairs for some peace and quiet.

She had frequented her local charity shop recently and found some wonderful books that she knew Evan would enjoy, one of them being Hans Christian Andersen's Book of Fairytales. There were many exciting stories inside. It was quite an old book, but still in good condition; she was going to enjoy reading them as much as Evan was going to enjoy listening to them.

There is nothing more magical than watching a child believing in the fantasy world of make-believe. Santa Claus, the Tooth Fairy, the Easter Bunny. Evan was going to be old enough this Christmas to be exceptionally excited.

It was sad, Sarah felt, that many parents nowadays didn't want or let their children hear the stories of generations past: the 'PC Brigade' who think it's wrong to let children believe in such falseness. Those who claim it inappropriate for the dashing prince to kiss Sleeping Beauty to awaken her from her hundred years' sleep having been cursed by an evil fairy. The stories had never harmed her, and yes of course she'd been devastated at the realisation that Santa Claus wasn't real; who wasn't? But oh, that joy of innocent wonder at the time.

"Ah, here's a nice story for you, Evan. 'The Emperor's New Clothes.' It's a funny one this is, and then tomorrow I'll read you 'The Steadfast Tin Soldier,' that's a little bit sad. Now then – "

"No, Grandad, read me the soldier story first. I want to hear that one, please."

Bill began to read the story and Evan was mesmerized. "Show me the pictures, Grandad."

Bill turned to the book to show him the coloured illustrations, "There's the soldier and there's his beautiful ballerina…"

Evan gasped and grabbed the book, holding it in front of his eyes, "Grandad!" He exclaimed excitedly, "look, he's the same as my dad when I was Eddie! Look, Grandad, he's got his uniform on with the big fluffy hat."

Bill was shocked, "Your dad, Evan?" Evan nodded, still looking at the picture with glee, and turned the pages. "Not my daddy Miles, my dad before."

He was saying it so matter-of-factly, as if Bill should know what he was talking about, then he passed the book back to Bill to continue the story. "He's in Heaven now though, Grandad. I miss him sometimes."

It was heartbreaking to hear such a little dot talk about missing someone. He thought back to that first day at nursery school when he'd asked the teacher to call his sister to come and fetch him. He was distressed and remained quiet for hours afterwards. What was going through his young mind?

Bill didn't know whether to push him further or leave it for Evan to lead. He checked the door to make sure Sarah wasn't standing outside. "Erm," he faltered, "Evan, were you here before? I mean, a long time ago?"

Evan looked into his eyes and nodded.

"And you were Eddie? Your name was Eddie, before?"

"Yes, Grandad, I was! I was Eddie when I was a man, but now I'm Evan."

Bill was excited. "And Jack Kowalski? He was your friend?"

Evan was thrilled, "Yes! We were rivals cos I was faster than Jack, Grandad. I beat him all the time and then after the war we... Oh, I don't want to talk anymore, Grandad. Can you go now? I don't want a story tonight."

Bill gave him a kiss on the forehead and left the room. "Night, night, sunshine. Sleep well."

But Evan didn't sleep well that night! Both Sarah and Bill went running into his bedroom an hour later as he was thrashing and screaming! They were concerned to see his face wet with sweat, his eyes wide open and yet not focusing on them. "Get down, get down, they're here, they're here, aarrrrrgh!"

"Evan, shhh, sweetheart, it's OK, I'm here. It's OK. Dad?"

"It's all right, Evan. You're safe now. Everything's all right. You can go to sleep now."

And just like that, the screaming and the thrashing stopped and Evan closed his eyes and continued breathing slowly.

Sarah and Bill left his room but left the door ajar in case he had another nightmare. Bill felt guilty; he felt his questioning might have triggered a past memory, but said nothing to Sarah for fear of being reprimanded.

Downstairs in the kitchen Bill put the kettle on to make them both a Horlick's drink. He was still feeling responsible for Evan's bad dream.

"I've read about children who have repetitive night terrors, Dad. Do you think I should talk to the doctor?"

"Well, it's hardly 'repetitive', Love. He's never had them before, so it's possible the lad just had a bad dream. All kids have them from time to time. It's natural. No point worrying unnecessarily, is there?"

Sarah nodded. Of course, her dad was right. "Did I have any nightmares like that then, that had you and Mum rushing into my bedroom or made you feel like I was missing something?"

"Not like that, no. You didn't scream or have nightmares, as such. It was just... Well, you used to get pretty upset sometimes and tell us about a girl who would come to you and sit on your bed."

"Sarah!"

"Yes," Bill reluctantly confirmed, "Sarah, I'd forgotten all about it until you mentioned it recently. You were adamant she couldn't be Sarah because you were her. Your mum believed... well, she liked to think, I should say that she liked to think it was your older sister.

Sarah frowned, "My sister?"

"Your mum miscarried after a few months. We never mentioned it to you because why would we? She always wanted a daughter to be named Sarah, so when you were born, you were Sarah. Sarah number two, I suppose? It gave your mum peace to hear you talk of the girl who sat on your bed talking to you. It made her feel that there was something after."

Sarah had no idea that her mother had had a miscarriage. "So there was a Sarah before, and a Sarah after, me?"

Bill nodded, "If you look at it like that, then yes." He was feeling extra brave now, "I suppose like Evan, really. He reckons he was Eddie before, and now he's Evan, Love," he reached out and took his daughter's hand in his, carefully thinking about his next words, "don't let's dismiss it. Sylvia says the lad has a past that we have no understanding about, but we need to hear him, support him record everything before he forgets it all, which he will. They all do."

Sarah felt he may be right! She'd done a brief search on the information her aunt had sent regarding Jack Kowalski.

He existed for certain, but Kowalski was a common name, there were hundreds and hundreds of them.

"Miles' parents are coming over tomorrow morning to have Evan for the weekend. Okay, Dad, we'll do it. But this is between you and me. Don't tell *anyone*."

23: AWOL

Bert Knifton breathed deeply as he arrived at last on British soil. He watched as his fellow citizens went about their day-to-day activities amongst the debris caused by the bombings. He figured he had a long walk to Leicestershire from London but he neither cared nor worried. He felt exhilarated, something akin to walking on air. He was free from the orders to kill, free from the stench of death. He felt liberated in the sense he'd made a drastic decision to do what he was doing, yet doubted his conscience would ever be free until he paid the price.

His only saving grace from his commissioned leave was that it was during the months of Spring, and that year the Lord had graced England with a warm one. He had no idea where he was going, and neither did he care. He would walk and walk until he recognised somewhere familiar.

The nights were cold, but he was used to cold. He would gaze up at the stars in the nighttime sky and shudder, knowing the nighttime sky is the same everywhere on earth, even in the trenches. How can such beauty and tranquility exist in such ugliness, side by side?

He didn't want to die; who did? But there was a limit to endurance. Pain was something too many people had to endure. He'd watched his comrades fall backwards into the trenches riddled with bullets, crying for their mothers and praying to God for salvation. He'd caused the same, on the other side. But now he was free. He had the letters in his pocket from Ed, the ones he was supposed to deliver to Ed's parents and his sister, the one who allegedly was going to be his future wife. Ha! As if that was ever going to happen.

He'd settled for the night aside a river. He figured if he kept close to the water's edge he would eventually arrive in Leicestershire. He could probably catch some fish to eat, snare a rabbit, eat berries. He didn't care... He didn't care. The taste of freedom alone was enough to sustain him.

Meanwhile, back in the trenches a week later, Patterson, Blythe, Hudson and Hurd were back. Knifton wasn't and that vexed Eddie. He worried every night, knowing full well Bert had been hinting at going AWOL. Absent Without Leave. Eddie prayed he'd never be found because that meant he'd surely face the firing squad. Every deserter knew that, too.

It's funny, Bert never considered himself a deserter of his position, his duty, more of a conscientious objector. He despised killing and yet acknowledged his need to kill to eat during his arduous trek back home. He'd never kill again, he convinced himself, he'd live on bread alone, potatoes and vegetables for evermore.

His heart lifted upon seeing the familiar roads leading to his home. He imagined the elation his family would extol upon him when he knocked, unexpectedly, upon the door, picturing their delighted faces with tears and joy and his mother's ecstatic embrace as she welcomed her beloved son home again. He could almost smell his father's familiar shaving cream, leaning his face next to his own in dire need of a shave.

He didn't knock on the door, there was no need. It was home. He turned the handle and walked in the front door like he'd only been gone a few hours. The smell that hit him was a blast of sweet nostalgia. It was his mother's perfume that she wore on rare occasions, it was her baking pastries, it was his siblings' nappies boiling on the copper... And then it turned to fear, acknowledgement that his life was now over.

The smell of defeat and hopelessness was devastating. The Military Police had been sitting waiting for him. There was no welcome from his mother, his father, only shame and disownment.

War was not only a term to describe battle fields, killing fields, for enemies to fight for control of what is sacred, it's also a place over the threshold where the unseen enemy is family... our very own nearest and dearest.

He couldn't cry, but he felt he wanted to. He was exhausted, mentally and physically. He had no idea how long he'd been walking but seeing his reflection in the window of his once so-called home, he knew he looked horrendous. A 'gentleman of the road' he felt. Unshaven, unwashed, unwelcome and unloved.

He relished the thought of facing the firing squad. It was a means to end all his woes and nightmares. He smiled reflecting on Tyler's premonition of marrying his sister, but according to him it wouldn't be the happiest of marriages. Albert had never even kissed a girl, and now he never would.

Before he was led away, he took out the notes Eddie had asked him to post to his family. He asked his mother to do this last thing for him.

"Don't look so smug, Knifton. We're taking you back. Can't afford to lose a good sniper as yourself."

That's when he broke down and all previous acts of bravado left him.

24: Evan

After his night of distress, Evan was nonstop chattering in the morning and he appeared to have had no memory of his nightmare terror, which was a huge relief for Sarah. In fact, he seemed ultra excited.

Sarah asked if he'd had a bad dream, but he denied it, replying that he'd had a good night. He continued by telling her he'd seen a man in his new story book that wore a big hat like his 'other daddy' used to wear. "Not my daddy Miles, Mummy, my daddy from before. He lives in Heaven, like Grandma Pat. And when I was Eddie and in Heaven, too, he showed me you, and told me I should chose you. Daddy John said you needed me."

Sarah was reeling, not quite knowing how to reply. She filled the milk jug from the carton in the fridge. She switched the kettle on to make another cup of instant coffee. "Your other daddy, Evan? You had another dad?"

Evan nodded whilst shoveling his cornflakes into his mouth. "Of course, Mummy! I had another daddy and mummy before I came down to you. Everybody does. I had my sister Meg like you had Sarah. I had three sisters and a brother, but Meg was my best sister. Johnny died as a baby."

Sarah sat with her coffee cup, joining Evan at the table. She remembered Mrs Evans, his nursery school teacher, asking if he'd been adopted because he was begging her to call his sister, Meg. *"Tell her it's Eddie,"* he said.

It had made Sarah feel a failure as a mother for her own child to implore his teacher to call someone she'd never heard of, to come to his aid. And Mrs. Evans, professional as ever, sometimes made Sarah feel as if she was hiding something.

"Evan, sweetheart, do you want to tell me? I mean... I don't understand, but I'm your mum and I'm here for you. You can tell me and your grandad anything."

Evan continued eating his cornflakes. "Bert should have been shot... but he wasn't. I was glad."

Who was Bert? She'd never heard that name before. Why was this person going to be shot and why was Evan glad he wasn't? She asked the questions, daringly.

"Oh, Mother. You're such a Scatterbrain. Have you forgotten it all, already?"

Scatterbrain! Again. And when had he ever called her *mother*? Where did he get it from? Certainly not from her nor Bill. "You have to stop using that word, Evan. It's not nice and I don't want to hear you saying again, do you understand?"

Evan pushed his empty cereal bowl forward, sighing heavily. He rose from the table, excusing himself. "No," he declared adamantly, "I'm four years old. I don't understand."

Four years old, plus a hundred or more. He had a wealth of history in his small memory bank. It needed to be told and heard.

Sylvia had now taken it upon herself to calling Bill regularly on his phone. Sometimes… no, more often than not, she would forget the time difference between Australia and England, and Bill would choose to ignore her early morning calls. They decided the most mutually acceptable way of communicating was via email or Messenger.

She felt she could confide in Bill whereas Bob was ambivalent. Bill, she felt, had more of a reason to listen to her.

"I'm sure I was 'here before,' too, Bill. It's taken me all these years to fully acknowledge it because it was never discussed in my day. Aren't we all guilty of brushing our pasts under the carpets? I want to know, now. I truly need to know because I want to make sense of it all. I can't sleep at night without hearing the screams in a dialect alien to me and yet it isn't at all. I'm glued to my iPad researches, every day.

"I think you really need to help Evan come to terms with his past life, like I said before, because he needs you to accept he has had a past life. I'm sure we all have, but most of us don't remember. How sad is that, Bill? How sad is it for all those like us who have forgotten? Is that how it's supposed to be? If it is, then why - as an adult - do I still feel a pull to the Isle of Skye?"

Many times, Bill inwardly cringed, didn't want to reply and yet felt curious at the same time. He knew Sylvia was right. He felt certain Evan's memories were real and that he'd been given another chance of life on Earth. It was beyond his, or anyone's, comprehension but couldn't think of any other explanation. Should he continue to delve or hope it would miraculously disappear?

He decided to take Sylvia's advice and make notes, keep a journal of sorts. He planned on setting up his camera to record their chats when they were alone at story time. He wanted to know more about his grandson's past, and he also wanted Sarah to be in agreement.

That night, Bill decided to set up his phone to record Evan's bedtime story. He was going to read him "The

Steadfast Tin Soldier," hopefully. He was already bathed and in his pajamas, eager to listen to his grandad read him a story.

"I'm ready now, Grandad," he said. "Last night I was sad because I hadn't seen my friend or my family for a long time and I wanted to go to sleep quickly so I could see him. Show me the pictures again."

Bill handed the book over so that Evan could study the colourful picture of the Tin Soldier in his red uniform with the huge black busby. He couldn't gauge what the boy was thinking and glanced up at his phone to ensure it was recording.

"Why has he only got one leg? Did he have an accident like Uncle Bob?"

Bill reassured him, "No, he didn't. He was made with only one leg because his creator didn't have enough metal left over to give him two legs. He made all the other soldiers and the ballerina though. They were all perfect. Do you want me to read you the story and you'll find out?"

Evan was studious for a moment. "But this soldier here, in the book, wasn't a proper soldier, was he, Grandad? He didn't fight in the war like me and Jack, did he? He was a soldier like my first daddy who just worked for the Queen at the castle. She liked him, my first daddy."

Now that was something entirely new to Bill, and Evan had just raised the goalposts! Bill was hoping his phone was recording this conversation because if he'd stupidly forgotten to press record, he was going to kick himself into Timbuktu!

"Tell me then, Evan. Tell your grandad cos I would really like to have known your other daddy. Miles was a lovely man; it's a shame you never got to meet him, and your other dad sounds like he had an interesting background too."

"Grandad!" Evan frowned, "Of course I met my daddy, Miles. I had two daddies in Heaven. Miles and John! They both looked after me. Grandma Pat looked after me, too. Meg, Silas, baby Sarah, everybody!"

Bill choked. "Silas?" he asked cautiously, "who's Silas?"

"Silas told me he didn't like how everyone called David 'Bobby'. He said it was cruel and he'd never call him Bobby. Silas told me he used to push you on the swing but once he pushed you too hard and went too high and then you fell off. You hit your face in the gravel and lost a tooth. Silas cried as he carried you home, but your mummy didn't forgive him. She does now though, Grandad. It was all *before*."

Bill swallowed deeply, he vaguely remembered that day at the park. He was what, three or four years old? David was backwards and forwards on the big slide, old enough to enjoy the features of the park without too much supervision, whilst Billy was just a toddler and his dad was attentive to fill the afternoon with happy memories.

Silas had placed Billy into the child's swing and fastened the wooden security prop in front and began pushing him from behind. Slowly, gently, and as young Billy squealed with delight, Silas became a little more earnest, pushing him higher as Billy shrieked with delight. Dawn was knitting yet all the time watching David, watching Silas with Billy.

Knit one, purl one, slip one over. The pattern was complicated and needed her full concentration. It was an Aran jumper for David. Once she'd finished it, she would make another one for Billy.

Bill could picture the scene as Evan described it. He was transported back to the park and felt the familiar feeling of the wind in his face as his father pushed him slowly at first, gradually getting faster and higher. It was the most bizarre feeling, seeing the sky and clouds as he tipped his head back laughing and laughing.

And then Dawn looked over to her husband, pushing her baby on the child's swing, and yelled in horror as she saw him soaring far higher than she felt was safe. "Silas!" She screamed, "not so high, for goodness' sake, he's a baby!"

In pure panic at hearing his wife's duress, Silas grabbed the back of the swing to slow it down but in doing so he brought it to an abrupt halt and young Billy fell over the wooden protective bar, head-first into the gravel... grazing his nose, chin, lips, and minus a tooth! Billy screamed like a banshee and Dawn was livid! She was absolutely furious with Silas for harming their child.

Evan watched his grandfather acknowledge the memory. "Is it nice to remember, Grandad? It doesn't hurt too much does it?"

Bill was dumbstruck. It was as if he'd watched it all over again on a huge TV screen, the memory becoming more and more crystal clear, like a glass of purified mountain water. He felt as inadequate and as juvenile as that small child swinging on a park swing just about to hit the deck and feel the impact as he fell headfirst on the ground. Thud, ouch!

He actually sensed the excruciating pain as he relived it all in slow motion. He covered his face with his hands as Evan watched him empathically. "Would you like to read me the story now, Grandad? Please?"

25: Meg

It was Saturday morning, and the shop was its usual hive of activity of weekend shoppers. Both May and Meg were backwards and forwards serving customers when a young woman intrepidly approached the polished wooden counter. She was dressed in a calf-length brown coat that was buttoned up to the neck and wore a matching hat with a brown leather handbag over her arm.

Meg was pouring a pint of vinegar into a bottle for a customer who declared she needed it for pickling some shallots. It was unusual to see a stranger in the shop. It was usually only the locals of the village.

May wiped her hands casually on her pinafore, "How can I help you?" she asked cheerfully.

"Are you Meg? I'm looking for a Mrs. Tyler and Meg. I have some letters for them."

May grabbed them and shouted to her mother to come to the shop. "Meg, quickly! They're from Eddie... and there's one for you. Look!"

Meg finished her task of filling the vinegar bottle and serving her customer without batting an eyelid or showing any surprise about the news of mail from their brother. There was a bucket of freshly cut Mimosa aside the barrel of vinegar, which their father had urged his daughters to sell quickly because he didn't know how long it would last once it had been cut. Mimosa was new, no one had ever seen it before and neither Meg nor May knew where their father had procured it from.

Annie rushed into the shop, glaring at the young woman in the brown coat who had brought precious news of her son. It was a very anxious moment because it was the first communication they'd received since he left.

"My brother came home on leave and he was supposed to deliver them himself, I'm led to believe, but... erm... well, he wasn't able to call himself so he asked if we would carry out his request. My mother would have liked to, truly, but she... well, she wasn't able. I hope you have good news. I must go now, goodbye."

As she turned to leave the shop, Meg called her back. "He's OK, you know. Albert. Please don't reject him or turn away from him. He's an incredibly brave man, you should be so proud."

Everybody in the shop fell silent as they watched Meg walk over and talk softly to the young lady in the brown coat

142

who began to sob silently. "How can you say that? Are you Meg? Is the other letter for you? Our family feel... disgraced. My parents can't..."

"You're Ivy, aren't you? Bert's sister? Don't worry 'Poison Ivy', he'll be back and he'll need you more than you will know."

The lady in the brown coat looked aghast. "What? What did you say? How did you... How did you know?"

Meg winked at her and took her hand, "I have a brother, too. Hang on, take a sprig of Mimosa, and please... write to him. He'll be waiting to hear from you."

The silence was then disturbed by Annie chastising Meg for talking a load of - what she considered - gobbledygook.

"Meg!" she stated very firmly, "we have other customers waiting to be served. Get a move on, for goodness' sake."

But the customers overhearing the incident between the young woman and Meg were piqued with curiosity. They all had male family members at war and were all waiting to receive letters. It was the not knowing, it was the hoping their prayers were being answered and their loved ones were being kept safe. Let it be happening to someone else, but not them. We're all guilty of wishing to be exempt of pain and heartache.

Mrs Brown hadn't heard from her Fred for months. She'd lost so much weight with the daily worry. She longed to see the postman yet dreaded it at the same time. She waited until Annie left the shop before daring to broach Meg.

"I haven't heard from Fred in such a long time now, Meg, I can't sleep, I can't... I want to believe..."

"Next week, Mrs. Brown. You'll receive a letter sometime next week. Fred's fine. Would you like to buy some mimosa? It's so pretty, isn't it?"

Gossip goes through a tight-knit village like Ibstock more quickly than a dose of Epsom salts when it's something that whips up a frenzy, and the Tyler shop on the High Street was becoming more and more patronised with most of the customers - still coming for their needed merchandise - yet not wanting to leave without having an opportunity of a one-to-one chance chat with Meg.

Annie was far from amused. "Should start charging the lot of them for the time she spends entertaining their silly fantasies. Damn those people in Manchester for putting her position on hold. It would be one less to mouth to feed and I wouldn't have to suffer the embarrassment of her sinister ramblings. Where did we go wrong with her, John? Why did we lose our beautiful Johnny and then have Meg to replace him?"

John was doing his ledgers and was niggled with the interruption from his wife. He also hated the connotations his wife was suggesting regarding his own secretly favoured daughter. His concentration was broken, again. He could continue his bookkeeping later.

"Love," he started, "Meg is a gift from Heaven above. We've been blessed and she herself has been blessed with a gift. It is so much more beyond our humble comprehension, but can you not see the joy she is bringing to those coming to her for answers? Shouldn't we be as proud of our young Meg as we are of Eddie? And indeed, all of our children?"

"But she's different, John! She's not the same as the others."

John laughed, agreeing. "Exactly. I grant you that. Meg is unique. Thank you, my dear, for giving me a child so unique. Now… let me read my son's letter in peace before I continue with the ledgers."

As John began reading the letter to the family, Meg was upstairs in her bedroom reading hers. It began, "To my dear skin and blister…" Meg smiled at her brother's use of their parents' much-used cockney colloquialisms.

She kept reading. "… as always you are right. How do you know all this stuff? How do you know it and we don't? I think you must have been a witch in a past life. Ha ha. I did meet Bert Knifton, as you predicted I would, and he's a really good man, Meg. You're going to be very lucky. Remember my friend Jack Kowalski? Can you believe he's here, too? We've met a few times. And yes, I'm in France. It's such a beautiful country, so big! I had no idea. It's so beautiful, Meg, I can't believe our Gt-grandparents ever wanted to leave. I think I might return one day, after this war is over. Want to come with me to find our roots? Shall we surprise Mum by visiting her kinfolk? Ooh, let's take her with us!"

Meg was saddened to realise that her brother could even contemplate such a trip in the future, knowing what she knew and that her brother had no inkling of. That being… their own mother's family were as dismissive to their own parent's marriage as Albert Knifton's were going to be to hers.

She began quickly scribbling a reply though she had no thoughts as to how her reply was going to reach her brother.

Right now, it didn't matter, it was just the importance of her need to jot down the words she needed to impart to him:

"*I will, once again, have the duty of polishing a trophy of yours and I will smile as I scrub away at the engraved letters of your name. Edward Tyler. Mother's first born and obvious favourite. I don't begrudge you that, brother, because you are mine, too. Rose was asking about you today, she's almost forgetting you. May hasn't heard from Will in over a year. She doesn't know how lucky she's going to be and neither does Will. Will's a nice man.*

"*Everything here remains almost the same but different. Ibstock is full of women and children nowadays. The church is never like it was before. It's morose, as the reverend reads out the names of the fallen. I don't go any more. I don't see the point.*

Albert's sister delivered your letters. I liked her but felt sorry for her. She's going to be torn. I supposed like our mother's sister was torn, with divided loyalties. Aren't families strange?

I would like to hope I've inherited our dear father's kindly nature rather than mother's and that I will love my children equally, and yet I'm sure it's natural to favour one more than another just as it's natural to favour one family pet over another. We can't help our feelings, can we?

I can't make my mind up who you take after, Eddie. Neither, in my opinion. You're free spirited, funny, and totally ugly! Rose definitely takes after our dad.

Please thank Bert for delivering your notes. It meant so much to us all.

Before I forget, I have to sadly you inform that Ivor Gimson's mother came into the shop a few weeks ago and announced that Ivor was 'missing in action'. Everybody dreads receiving such a telegram, but Mrs. Gimson is adamant it's all a big mistake and that he's most likely only wounded and recuperating in a hospital somewhere. He isn't, but if that gives her an iota of comfort, then so be it. Who am I to be the bearer of such tragic news?

I was delighted to read you have seen your friend Jack, again. I'm sure you must have had lots to talk about and enjoyed your usual witty banter. I will look forward to meeting him one day when our countries will once again be a safe haven and our menfolk are not forced to kill another human-being purely because they're told to do so by elders who sit around a huge polished table, drinking Brandy, smoking their fat expensive cigars, whilst making all the wrong decisions.

Well, brother dearest, I will finish now. This dreadful war drags on and on with so much unnecessary devastation, loss and sadness and much more to come.

Know that we keep you in our prayers and thoughts every day, all of you.

Your ever-loving sister,

Meg"

"Rudi, here's a ha'penny. Can you take this letter for me? It's to go to my brother who's fighting in France and if I receive news back from him then I'll know you did a good job and I'll give you a penny-mouthful of ice-cream but it's our secret, Rudi, so don't tell a soul. Can I rely on you?"

Rudi was nine-years old and had only once had a dib of his finger into the delicious ice-cream that was being made at the shop in the High Street. A penny-mouthful of the cold creamy nectar was too tantalising a reward to mess up. He ardently promised, crossing his heart for total confirmation, and four months later nine-year-old Rudi Bourne walked proudly upright down Ibstock High Street savoring his very own dish of heaven, surrounded by a crowd of envious on-lookers.

Eddie had received her letter, and she'd received her reply.

26: Evan

Bill had watched the recording he'd made of Evan's memory the night he'd set up the camera in his bedroom. He'd watched it over and over and over. He watched his own facial reactions as his four-year-old grandson described the time his father pushed him on the swing while his mother was knitting, and his brother was on the big slides.

There was no way on God's earth Evan could have known all that! He'd even forgotten it himself, until he was transported back in time. He acknowledged that Sylvia was dead right: reincarnation must be real!

He'd sent her the recording and she had been equally excited. The two of them were developing a closer relationship and understanding of each other. She would tell him of her findings, and he would reciprocate.

Bill had become so eager to continue his filming sessions every night and felt guilty that he'd not yet decided to include Sarah until he had enough evidence to convince her, until this one particular night when she casually announced she'd join them in the storytelling.

The camera was already set up and Bill was praying she wouldn't notice. Sarah lay on the bed, cuddling Evan, waiting for the storytelling to begin. She was excited to see how her son was enjoying the new book she'd bought when out of the mouths of babes, Evan went into full throttle and more.

"It's our special time now, Mum, for Grandad and me. I go to sleep and I can see me again when I was before I was your baby. I see my other daddy and Meg again. Tell her, Grandad. Tell her you know."

Evan and Sarah were looking at Bill for that confirmation as Bill began opening the book, searching to find something to read, feeling their eyes on him, waiting for an answer.

"Grandad fell out of the swing and hurt his tooth, didn't you, Grandad?"

Bill laughed nervously. He couldn't deny what his grandson had said but he didn't know how to continue. And then he closed the book giving a big sigh of defeat. He looked at Evan's anticipating face, knowing he had to come clean and admit… something.

"I never did tell you how your Uncle Bob got his name, did I?"

Sarah raised her eyebrows in humorous confusion. What did he mean? She had no reason to question he was anyone other than her Uncle Bob.

"His Christian name is David. Dave to us, until the day he disgraced himself at the park, decades ago when he became Bobby to everyone."

Evan was now leaning forward with an all-knowing glint in his eye as he watched his grandfather relay the story, cringingly. Sarah had never known this story and screeched with laugher.

"Oh, poor Uncle Bob, why did he keep that dreadful nickname after they emigrated to Australia? Surely he could have introduced himself as Dave?"

Bill nodded in agreement, "Except that Sylvia met him as Bob, so she could never think of him as being Dave.

Evan leapt in then, "It's the same for me, Grandad. I was Eddie before and now I'm Evan, so I have two names, too. Just like Uncle Bob." He turned to Sarah, "Do you remember who you were before, Mum?"

His face was beseeching her to tell but Sarah was trying to digest the statement he'd just uttered. She looked imploringly to her dad, once again aghast at the words from her young son's mouth. She considered - in the fraction of thought - whether to humor him and play along with the storytelling and invent something to amuse him.

Everybody likes some kind of fantasy, make-believe, whether you're four-years old or ninety, and Sarah wanted to humor her boy.

"Oh, indeed I was, young man! I was once a very beautiful and desirable Princess, I'll have you know. Prince Miles was so besotted with my beauty he begged me to marry him and live happily ever after in his magnificent castle. We danced to the best musicians in the world and the colourful jesters entertained us nightly. We drank the finest wines and feasted upon the fatted calf. The merriment continued…"

"And then Mile's got poorly, didn't he Mum?" He finished off her sentence.

Sarah nodded, remembering tenderly, reiterating Evan's words, "Then Miles got poorly. He did, Evan. He got very poorly and then he got called up to go to Heaven where he is now, but we loved each other dearly for the time we were allowed, and I have no regrets whatsoever."

"Now," Evan said, reaffirming his mother's words, "he's in Heaven now, but then he might come back again, if he wants to, if he's done enough."

Bill was hoping his battery was going to last long enough to record the night's chitchat. "Evan," he said, "shall I read you a story or would you like to tell us one of yours?"

Evan was surprised at his grandad's request. He'd always loved to listen to a story but now - looking at his mother's and grandfather's anticipatory faces, could see their eagerness, too.

He sat upright in his bed, plumping up the pillow to support him, and turned to Sarah. "Mummy," he began, "can I tell you my story about when I used to be Eddie?"

"Of course you can, sweetheart. We'd love to hear all about it, but wait a moment, Evan. I'll just fetch my iPad so we can record it for us to watch later."

Bill sighed with relief.

27: Back in France

No amount of cajoling from Eddie was lifting Bert's spirits. He'd said little since being marched back to Hell. He performed his deadly duties robotically, perfunctorily, emotionlessly. It was as if he was picking them off, one by one, eliminating as many as possible, eradicating the whole damn war problem so there would be no one left to kill. Load, seek, aim, fire. Repeat. Repeat.

He blinked endlessly to discharge his tears that clouded his vision. He was no coward and yet the bravest thing he could do was to end the nightmare by shooting himself. *That* he couldn't do. Oh, he'd considered it every single day but then he knew he would be passing the buck to another, and he wasn't prepared to shift his conscience to someone else.

"Do you ever keep count, Bert?" Eddie's words haunted him every day. There was a count, a number somewhere, but Albert Knifton would never know.

It was mid afternoon and eerily quiet. Eddie had just finished writing his letters to his family. He looked around for Bert but couldn't see him so decided to have a wander, exchanging simple greetings with his comrades on his journey. He passed the wounded and envied some of the lesser injured as they were considered the lucky ones and would be soon on the home run, back home to Blighty and their families.

Meg had told him that he would return, get to win another trophy, but what if she was wrong? What if God had other plans for him? He'd actually been quite blasé about his good fortune and was confident enough in his sister's predictions to believe he would indeed return unscathed.

She'd also told him he would meet her future husband, and he did! How did she know everything like she did and why did their mother discourage her so? Was she clairvoyant? Psychic? Or just lucky with her guesswork? Why had his sister been given this gift and no one else had?

Poor Meg, he suddenly acknowledged. If it was all true, and she knew so much about what was going to happen then she must also know the about bad stuff that was going to happen, too, like the time the pianist chap came to their village and she'd declared "He's going to regret coming to Ibstock".

Meg, Eddie realised, was often being scolded by their mother for her ramblings, as she called them, which must have been dreadful for her to have to say nothing about what she felt was true!

"You'll meet Albert Knifton, my future husband, but it won't be a happy marriage." Her words saddened Eddie because his favourite sister deserved to have a happy marriage, and Bert definitely needed to have a happy life after this atrocity and felt sure Meg would be the perfect wife for him. She would be the perfect wife for anyone, and he hoped he would be lucky enough to meet someone a fraction as good as her. What made the young girl say or think she wasn't going to be happy?

She never told Eddie he was going to be married or have a happy life, only that she would have another trophy to polish. Perhaps, he thought, she couldn't see that far ahead, and that was fine with Eddie because he was too focused on his future as a cycling champion. He dreamt of returning to France again to compete in the Tour de France, if it was going to continue afterwards.

He'd read about it in his father's newspapers and saw no reason why he and Kowalski shouldn't be there, together, racing up to the finishing line filled with adrenaline, pushing his legs harder and harder, feeling the pain and sweat running down his body, trying to ignore hearing his heartbeat thudding with anticipation amid the cheering of the crowd... And he could see it all: the finishing line was a euphoric sight

- in his imagination - he'd look behind and see Jack and he'd raise his middle finger.

"In your dreams, Kowalski. In your wildest dreams."

He passed Colonel Rogers playing a game of cards with a soldier who was bandaged around the knee, the lower part of his leg missing. One of the lucky ones now destined to go home.

He passed a group of older guys, smoking and talking nonsense.

He noticed a couple of younger kids huddled together in a corner, then looked away. He wasn't one to judge.

He walked looking and looking away, and then he heard something like singing! Not joyous singing, not a hymn or a recognised song, it was more of a lament, a dirge. And then he saw Bert on all fours, with his hands clasped together in prayer. He took a sharp step backwards because he felt he was intruding on an extremely personal moment. He held his breath because the mere act of breathing was bound to be heard, and he tiptoed backwards, respectfully.

Nighttime fell and still there was an unnerving silence that permeated the trenches. Colonel Rogers was left wondering if the opposition had run out of ammunition.

They had some, enough for however long enough was going to last. Was this the proverbial lull before the storm scenario? It was mind games, trying to outwit each other with no answers at all.

Rogers walked up and down, counting his men, assessing their capabilities and their dispensability. It was a despicable position he was in, but someone had been commissioned to do the dastardly deed.

He glanced over to Tyler who was sitting next to Knifton, both much valued men he couldn't wager losing. He looked at the pitiful tormented faces of young and old and tried not to see them as human beings with families who yearned to feel them in their arms again. He needed to choose but damned if he could.

He walked along the trenches picking up bits of grass, the few that had miraculously managed to push up and thrive. Two used match sticks he found, and three blades of grass. Five options. The one who drew the shortest, was the unlucky winner.

Young James drew the shortest straw and looked to his friend in bewilderment. Eddie had seen the youngsters earlier, huddled together, and knew neither of them were capable of being heroes.

"You forgot to include ours, sir." Eddie stood up, "I believe it is I who have drawn the shortest straw. Look, it is smaller than a fingernail, much smaller than that of James'."

Colonel Rogers squinted at the proffered piece of debris being held high in Tyler's fingers, knowing full well he not been given one. He was annoyed because Tyler had other duties he needed to fulfill and there was nobody remotely capable of filling his boots. What to do now?

He had no alternative other than to accept the challenge and knew that Tyler knew it, too.

"Follow me," Rogers ordered sternly. He was not amused!

"You and your friend, Kawasaki, you're both needed because – "

Eddie suddenly realised in a moment or pure disbelief. The penny dropped loud and sadly too clear. Kowalski versus Kawasaki. It was an easy mistake to make but a worrying one, nevertheless, with dire consequences.

"Kowalski, sir. Kawasaki is a Japanese engine manufacturer. Jack Kowalski is a dear friend of mine."

Rogers could have bitten off his tongue. "Kawasaki? Kowalski? Same difference. Anyway, you blithering idiot, what in God's name possessed you to pull a ludicrous stunt like that? I'm the decision maker in these unfortunate circumstances, not you, but seeing as though you've presented me with a problem I can't escape from, you've left me with no choice. Strewth man, you and Knifton cause me some very unnecessary headaches."

"James is too young to act the hero, with respect, sir. I'm more than – "

"He's a *man*, therefore old enough to do his duty for King and Country the same as everyone else here. Good grief, Tyler, do you think I enjoy having to choose the unfortunate bugger who's dispensable? My grandson's but a year or two younger than that boy and would I send him over the top? No, of course, I wouldn't, but we're at war and such decisions - right or wrong - need to be made."

Rogers took out his silver hip flask, needing to calm himself, and took a swig. He looked at the initials on the front; it had been his father's. He proffered it to Eddie, "I can't lose you, Tyler. I'll have Knifton cover you. At least you'll have half a chance. Damn and blast you, Tyler. Damn and bloody blast you."

"So," said Eddie, numbly, "I'm going over?"

Rogers couldn't answer him. He didn't want to discuss anything with him at the time because he felt too depleted. "Later. We'll talk about your orders, later."

Bert had a small harmonica that he'd been given as a birthday present from his parents, as a young boy. He loved the musical instrument though played it infrequently, yet as Eddie returned to join the crowd awaiting his news, he heard the melodic tune of 'A Bird in a Gilded Cage' and suddenly felt uplifted and fearless. All eyes turned to Eddie as he sang along - in a masculine voice - to Bert's rendition.

How many times had he heard Meg sing the very same song? Is this what she meant? Was she destined to be the bird in a gilded cage?

'She's only a bird in a gilded cage, a beautiful sight to see.

You may think she's happy and free from care.

She's not, though she seems to be.'

In the trenches, there was no distinction of wealth. Perhaps her Bert was affluent, Eddie didn't know.

As Eddie crouched down next to Bert, Bert stopped playing and looked at him, waiting for an answer to a question no one had dared - yet - to ask. He looked at all the anticipatory faces; James, Albert, Hurd, Staniforth, Machin, Boswell, and burst out laughing.

"My sister's favourite Song. Funny you should play that, hey, Knifton?" The innuendo was lost on their comrades/the audience, so Eddie decided to educate them.

"My younger sister has the voice of an angel. In fact, I think she could actually be an angel." He turned his head directing his speech to Albert, "When she was about six or seven years old, I can't truly remember now, but she was singing in church. It was midnight mass, Christmas. Compulsory attendance in our house. Anyway, my sister, Meg, sang Silent Night."

No one moved a muscle as they all leaned in to listen to Eddie talk of his sister. He was good with words and loved an attentive audience. His face was aglow with pride as he recounted the memory.

"I'm telling you, guys, I had goosebumps all up my arms as I listened to my baby 'skin and blister' sing her little heart out and I wanted to rush over, pick her up, and swirl her round and round because I was sooooo proud of her."

He tipped his head back as if to see it happening above him. "Play it, Bert. I want to hear it again."

Bert took up his harmonica and played it again. "She was wearing her brown pinafore dress which was not befitting attire for an angel. May and Rose, my other sisters, were different. They were treated differently. My mother, too. She had a silver fox fur over her shoulders, and I remember watching Meg sing... sooo confidently as if she'd been singing opera songs her whole life."

Bert was still playing quietly now but had his ear to Eddie's story. "There was a couple at the church that Christmas, some Italian folk, and when they heard our Meg sing they wanted to take her back to Italy to have her voice properly trained so she could become a proper singer. I mean, she *was* a proper singer, but she was just a kid."

Eddie frowned, realising the chance denied to her by the very mother who made arrangements for her to be deployed to Manchester!

"This couple, these Italians, came to the shop and asked my parents' permission to become her legal guardians so that they could look after her and make her something. Something people would want to pay money to listen to her sing. Families, hey men? My mother refused so poor Meg never got her one and only chance of success."

Bert had stopped playing his harmonica. "You should have been a writer instead of a cyclist, Tyler, or an artist, for you paint a pretty picture, I'll grant you that. Why are you so obsessed with your sister? Is there something you'd like to tell us? Give us a reason to laugh, maybe?"

Instead of showing shock, Eddie decided not to retaliate. "I believe you had a similar bond with your own sister, did you not, Bert? Wasn't it Ivy who went against your own parents in your defense?"

Bert was livid. His so-called friend had just highlighted his shame amongst the whole troop and no one, ever, had dared even hint at it since his return. He put his harmonica in his trench coat pocket, rose from his sitting position, and walked away.

James looked to Eddie sheepishly and waited until everyone had dispersed. He knew, as did they all, what Eddie had done. "Eddie," he kinda stuttered, "I know that a thank-you will never be enough, but it's all I have. My heartfelt thank you and this… it's my sister's lucky locket. She had it made especially… I love my sister too. Please take it, it's brought me good luck so far and so it's passed to you now. If you open it you will see us, Winnie and me. See?"

Eddie opened the locket and saw the mirror image of siblings. "She's my twin sister. A nurse. When this is over, will you find her and... well... will you find her for me, please?"

Eddie nodded, looking at the juvenile smiley faces in sepia, "I will," he said, "and when you return, she can hand it back to you."

Rogers now had the unpleasant task of giving Eddie his orders. He'd slept fitfully that night, the dawn of the morning as unwelcome as an erection in a whorehouse at the end of a busy Saturday night. It was 7.00 a.m. and damned if Tyler wasn't already outside, shaved, and ready whereas he was still wearing underwear that had seen much better days, dithering...

"These are your orders, Tyler, but I'll say it again, I'm most displeased at your foolhardiness. The short straw was not your decision to call."

Eddie smiled, "Seems it was after all, sir. You can't change destiny. Please tell Knifton to watch my back. How many grenades have I?"

"Four."

"Only four? I want three more. Seven's my lucky number."

There had been nothing from the opposition in days. It was scarily quiet as if they'd all decided to flee and perhaps they had. Eddie was creeping alone into territory he had no knowledge of. He'd climbed the ladder that had him now above the trenches, not an unfamiliar sight but this time it felt different. He was alone for one thing.

He slithered forwards slowly, until eventually encountering rotting limbs, bits of flesh and bone, and dared not look at their decay in case he should vomit. The smell was unbearable. Why had no one taken their dead away? Perhaps they had but not all of their body parts.

Each agonising move forced him to remember his task and he clutched the grenades for reassurance, his finger interlocking the trigger… readying. There was nothing there. It was totally void of any human activity. Eddie sighed with relief and wanted to laugh thinking that young James would have had his opportunity to be a hero after all, until his euphoria was shattered by an ear-piercing screech of a bullet passing his head and the feeling of warm blood over his face. In front of him, not a meter away, he saw the fear on a face of some German he would never not see again… now it lay face down in the mud.

He rolled over on his back, panting loudly, gasping for breath, wondering how many more there were, watching him, realising he wasn't alone. He stayed low for seconds, minutes, he didn't know. He wanted to extend his hand in a wave to Bert; he was doing what he'd been ordered to do: cover him.

Eddie rolled back again onto his stomach, surveying how much further he had to go. He was filled with dread as he made his first crawling movement, inching his way on his elbows.

Another whizz of a bullet and another yelp before the silence. Bert was indeed a crack shot. It was instant death for his targets. Two down…

Foolhardy was the description Rogers had used to describe him. Brave was James'. Eddie laughed at himself: Rogers was more correct. Only an idiot would have volunteered for this ridiculous mission. There was no way he was going to be able to complete his task and come out of it alive. His parents would be among the many to receive the dreaded telegram and his name read out in church, like so many others. He concluded his sister was wrong but by crikey he'd try his best to make them all proud.

His dreams of winning the Tour de France in time to come were just that: a foolhardy dream! He hoped Jack would remember him and as *he* passed the finishing line would raise *his* middle finger and shout, "In *your* wildest dreams, Tyler!"

He was actually still laughing at his thoughts when suddenly he saw a German helmet move in a wooden parapet ahead. His pulse accelerated and he pulled the grenade's pin and threw it as hard and as accurately as he could. He lay flat to the ground, covering himself.

The blast was deafening. The screams blood-curdling. Three, four, five shots pealed the air. He covered his head with his hands. He had six more grenades and utilised a second. Nothing. No screams, just the echo of the grenade's explosion.

Where were they all?

Eddie Tyler never considered himself hero material. He was a fair-weather cyclist in his spare time, and a simple journalist by day. If he could have made his living by cycling alone, he would have given his eyeteeth, but getting the local gossip at least paid his board and lodgings. There was not much reporting to be done in his little village nor indeed the neighbouring ones but everyone seemed to want to know who was getting matched, hatched, or despatched.

People. They have this in-built curiosity to know what's happening in everybody else's lives. Nosey Parkers, curtain twitchers, even Peeping Toms. It was easy money for him, truth be told. Reports on local football teams' accolades, announcing bingo winners, who produced the biggest onions at the County Fair, and whose flippin' budgie died due to a chimney fire! 'Poor Joey' was the embarrassing title. What complete and utter humiliation was that? It was even more embarrassing because it was the damned budgerigar of his own sister Rose!

And yet he acquiesced everyone had their secrets or tried to conceal them. Eddie knew an awful lot about an awful lot of people.

He lay for the longest time, trying not to move a muscle. He was on his back again, looking upwards to the sky. He knew he was being watched, at least from his own side. He pictured them all anxiously looking over, armed and ready to back him up. He wondered how young James would have done, if he hadn't stepped up.

The silence continued. There was nothing, but even nothing sounded terrifying, so he lay there…

He had no idea of time or how long he'd waited. The sun was now shining so he considered this a good omen and decided to move again, inching forwards on his arms as he'd done previously. Closer and closer to the parapet, with his third grenade ready.

Eddie risked a slight glance backwards hoping Bert was still watching. Of course he would be. Eddie pushed his upper body up, slowly, slowly, hardly daring to draw breath or exhale. It was now he absolutely needed Bert's expertise as a crackshot sniper because otherwise he was history!

He sighed slowly and silently as he assessed his assignment and moved away the bloody remains of the enemy in charge of the Gatling gun. He stood up in front of it, knowing Knifton would see him and gave a thumbs up. Rogers was correct in his calculations that the majority had moved on and left their own 'dispensables' to keep up an appearance and prolong the agonies.

This was a victory, in his opinion. They could all pack up and move, perhaps go home. They could declare this battle won and it would be a joyous and much deserved celebration. Albert could play some jovial music on his harmonica, and everyone would join in, dancing and rejoicing.

Eddie lifted the Gatling Gun to the skies and fired off a short round, knowing it would be seen, but his euphoria and self-satisfaction was short lived when he heard a cry behind him and he froze... He was another disposal, like James. Another youngster, left behind trembling and petrified.

Eddie could have considered using another of his grenades and diving out of harm's way, but he was a human being, faced with another terrified human being.

"Bitte, bitte nicht." (Please, please don't.). The boy had wet himself in fear.

"Viens," Eddie offered truthfully, hoping his French would be interpreted by the young German, *"C'est fini!"* (Come. It's over.)

The young German appeared to be relieved and didn't hesitate to follow him. He most probably knew that even being taken prisoner would be a safer alternative.

The boy was blond and blue eyed, a typical German youth, exactly the same as young James. (Not at this time a *Lebensborn*, but an earlier version.)

The fact that Eddie's captive walked upright, willingly beside him back to British trenches, gave him the confidence there would be no more blood to be spilled. It was over for him and indeed for most.

There was loud rejoicing as they got nearer and nearer and suddenly Eddie and his prisoner - of whom he hadn't yet asked his name - were scrambled upon, hugged, kissed, slapped, and led back down. Suddenly those muddy, stinking, abysmal trenches felt like home... It felt safe.

Karl. His name was Karl. The only difference between Karl and James and many others was that Karl had been born in Germany and therefore would thereinafter be considered the enemy. A threat and a dangerous person.

Eddie needed time alone with Albert to thank him for saving his life. He hadn't been there with the others, and he understood.

It was a different melodic tune he heard now. Albert could play anything and everything on his harmonica and he sat back joining the crowd as they clapped and swayed to his musical entertainment.

It would be his last moment of seeing Bert so carefree and almost happy, because even though Eddie had done his bit for the war effort, he'd other duties to fulfill that he didn't know about!

"Tyler," Rogers shouted loudly. "Come."

28: Evan, Collette, Sarah, and Bill

Evan's nursery teacher, Mrs. Evans, had been hard to convince that her young scholar had not been adopted. From his first day when he'd begged her to call his sister to come to collect him, to numerous others when he'd talk about his 'other mummy' and his family who he missed. It wasn't until later when he spoke of his friend, Jack, and how he would tell his fellow class mates that it didn't matter if they died because they would all have the opportunity to slide down the 'beautiful tunnel' and be born again, that she began to reconsider.

Evan was a character and a half and as he grew older, the more knowing he became.

"Mrs. Evans," he said to her one day when she was not paying attention to the classroom full of toddlers but looking on her phone, "Matthew's still here. He's with you every day. You shouldn't miss him… he's happy now."

She looked aghast at the young boy looking at her with the most compassionate expression. Matthew! The absolute love of her life who took his own life and she would never in a million years understand why.

"He didn't want to make you sad, but he was sad and that's why he wanted to go, but he's OK now, and he says you need to be, too. It's OK, Mrs. Evans, because Matthew will come back again one day. We all do. All of us."

And so, Collette Evans, too, wondered about this special little boy in her classroom. Had he 'been here before'? She was well aware that kiddies come out with the strangest things but how could he have possibly known about her Matthew? They weren't even from Leicestershire: she'd left Ireland about twelve months after her husband's suicide, wanting an escape, away from all the painful memories.

Collette wanted to sob at hearing the words of reassurance from such a little treasure and glanced around to make sure the rest of the children were engaged in some activity before walking over to sit next to him. She picked up a piece of the jigsaw puzzle he was doing, looking to see if she could place it somewhere. Evan often sat alone and it gave her the opportunity to spend a little time with just him. He beamed at her when he saw her sitting with him and studied the piece in her fingers.

"It's OK, Mrs. Evans, you can ask me," he said, glancing to the top right of the puzzle.

Once again Collette wondered how he knew the reason she approached him.

"It goes here, look, at the top."

"How do you know, Evan?"

"Because it has the wing of the airplane."

Collette, laughed, "No, not the jigsaw piece, how do you know about..." She still stumbled whenever Matthew's name was on her lips.

He rested his chin on his hand, leaning on the table, scanning the pieces. It wasn't a huge puzzle, only twenty pieces. "Because I was there before I was me. You know."

She shook her head, "No, I don't know. Do you want to tell me?"

Evan looked stunned at her reply, "Mrs. Evans!" he exclaimed, "But you're the teacher!"

Trying hard not to laugh again, she continued, "Oh, Evan, we teachers don't know everything, and I'm certain you could definitely teach me a thing or two. So... you said you were here before you were you? Where were you?"

"Heaven," he answered matter-of-factly, "when I was Eddie, because I died and then I then I had to go to live in Heaven."

"You died?" Collette gasped. Evan nodded, picking up some more pieces of the jigsaw puzzle. "Yes, in France, I got shot."

"Oh, Evan, I'm so sorry, that's so sad."

"Everybody was sad but I wasn't because nobody gets sad there. Matthew isn't sad either, only you. He's happy now because it's nice in Heaven, Mrs. Evans, don't you remember?"

She wanted to hug him so tightly but she knew she shouldn't. She truly hoped that Matthew was at peace, like this child was telling her he was. Didn't everyone who lost a loved one hope for the same, if indeed it was true? It was a reassuring thought.

She was just about to ask more questions as she had this dire need to know more, but the clock on the wall told her it was 3.30 p.m. and parents would be waiting outside to collect their children.

"Thank you, Evan. Bless your little heart."

*   *   *   *   *

Sarah loved this time of day when she met Evan out of his classroom, dying to hear all about his day. She was slightly concerned that he always left the room alone, as if

180

he hadn't yet made any friends. She watched groups of girls and boys depart together, holding hands, their voices loud with excitement, but not her son.

She'd asked him on a couple of occasions if he actually played with anyone, if he had his own special friend, and he'd just shake his head, which disappointed her. Nobody likes to contemplate their child as friendless, and she couldn't comprehend him not having any when he was so knowledgeable. Perhaps he was too advanced for his peers and they couldn't keep up?

But this afternoon he walked out of his classroom smiling and instantly Sarah felt uplifted. He was accompanied by Mrs. Evans, who greeted Sarah enthusiastically.

"Can I just tell you what a little darling you have here, Sarah?" Collette said, looking down on Evan adoringly. They both looked at Evan who was looking back at them. "He's a credit to you and… and… well, I believe he's one exceptional child."

The two ladies held each other's gaze for a second longer than was normal and Sarah seemed to feel the teacher was trying to convey something.

"We know," she answered. "We're very lucky to have him, aren't we, Sweetheart?"

"Do you… would you be able to spare me a minute or two, if you don't mind?" Collette asked softly. "I don't want to keep you, but I…"

Sarah's forehead creased in concern, feeling a little apprehensive. "Is everything alright, Mrs. Evans? He hasn't done anything wrong, has he?"

"Wrong? Oh my word, not at all, he never does anything wrong. I wish they were all as well behaved as Evan, no, please come back inside for a moment. Evan, would you like to sit at your jigsaw for a second while I have a quick chat with your mummy?"

They returned to the classroom and Evan went straight back to the puzzle while Sarah sat opposite Collette.

"Does this have something to do with him wanting you to call his sister, from before?"

Collette collected her thoughts and began. "I was born in Ireland, you probably guessed by my accent. I moved to Leicestershire six years ago after I lost my husband."

"Oh, I'm so sorry!"

Collette shook away her condolences, "Today, your son said something to me which has given me a great amount of comfort." She paused, waiting for Sarah to acknowledge her

182

words. "He told me Matthew was happy now and I shouldn't miss him. Matthew is my husband. Very few people know I'm a widow. I thought… earlier when he said he was Eddie before, that maybe you had adopted him, but… he isn't adopted is he, Sarah? He really has been here before?"

"Finished!" Evan shouted with pride, interrupting the two ladies, "I've finished the puzzle. Look, Mum! I did it all by myself."

Sarah looked back to answer Collette, "We don't know, Mrs. Evans. How can we? I agree with you that he is an exceptional child, thank you, and I'm pleased he was able to give you some comfort. My father and I are still trying to process everything we're learning about what he tells us at home. We're keeping notes and we intend doing some research but it's all too vague at the moment."

She rose from her chair to leave, "Have you ever been to France?" Collette asked.

Sarah shook her head, confused.

"Evan has" Collette said, " he told me he died there."

* * * * *

"What took so long?" Bill asked when they eventually got to the car and buckled up. "I was just about getting ready to come and look for the pair of you."

Sarah told her dad that the teacher wanted to have a quick chat about his progress, and she'd tell him more, later. Bill read between the lines and said no more.

After Evan's routine nightly bath and he was sitting up in bed, Bill got out the story book. He'd read most of the stories now and was turning the pages to try to find a new one.

"Grandad, you know the solider with one leg?" Bill nodded. "Read it again, please?"

Bill was reluctant to read the story yet again as he'd read it many times already. He thought about inventing a few different scenarios or making something up to relieve the tedium, so he looked on his phone to see how he could ad-lib, when he came across an article about a cartoon adaptation on the original storyline by the original illustrator of Hans Christian Andersen.

The cartoon version plot was altered so that the antagonist was not actually the Jack-in-the-Box, but a King who wanted the ballerina all for himself. The tin soldier - seething with jealousy - attacked his competitor and as a result was put on trial and sentenced to death… via the firing squad.

The ballerina pleaded with the King to spare him, but her pleas were denied and so she chose to stand beside her beloved tin soldier where they were both executed. When they landed in the burning fire, they melted together into a heart shape and went to toy heaven where they lived happily ever after.

Evan was very contemplative. He was thinking about the different version of the story, deeply.

"He upset the King because the King gives the orders and the tin soldier knew that he would get shot but was willing to disobey him because he wanted to be free?"

Bill agreed, "That was just a variation on the real story, the first one. And then the tin soldier got his missing leg fixed in toy heaven, so he became as perfect as his perfect ballerina."

Evan was still digesting this news. "Bert should have faced the firing squad too, Grandad, but the King didn't let him. And it's true, God fixes everything when you go to live in Heaven. My daddy Miles isn't poorly anymore, and Grandma Pat is young again. Heaven is like a magic place isn't it?"

Bill was speechless… again! "Evan, Son, I've heard you mention Bert before… but who is he?"

"Oh, Grandad. Of course, you know who Bert is! He used to give Grandma Pat a penny every Friday for her pocket money."

29: Pawns

There was much merriment and relief in the trenches as the soldiers dared to consider it may all be over for them. More cigarettes were smoked, more letters home were being written, less prayers were sent Heavenward.

"This should be your last mission, Tyler. And yes, thank you for all you did yesterday. You will get a medal, and well deserved too! We're packing up and hope to be moving on imminently, but you have tonight to do before we can put this bloody episode behind us. This package is for the normal drop off, and this is for Kawasaki."

"Kowalski, sir."

"Kowalski, yes, pardon me. Travelling by nighttime should be safer, seeing as the cowards have fled, but take nothing for granted. They're cunning buggers, so heed my words. Be back as swiftly as possible, do you hear me? No dallying with your friend."

Eddie couldn't shake off the Colonel's mistake between his friend's surname and the Japanese engine company. He acknowledged the similarity but couldn't understand how he had confused the two unless something had triggered his memory.

Not only that, but neither he nor Jack knew the purpose of their rendezvous. Their packages were sealed anyway. They never saw anyone from the derelict farmhouse, they never met anyone on route either.

He left under a glowing red sky and felt no fear as the route was familiar to him now. However, he knew the Germans had left and could be close, or miles away.

France was so vast! Miles and miles of absolute nothingness other than miles and miles of more open space. There was no hiding place and yet he felt sure some must have sought refuge somewhere.

It was the smell of burning he noticed first. Smoke. Not an ignited cigarette, more wood burning. He stopped peddling and rested his feet on the ground.

"Tyler" he heard his name whispered. "Tyler, we're here."

"*We?*" Eddie wondered, "*who else was with Jack?*"

Eddie suddenly saw a cigarette burning and dismounted his paltry excuse for a bicycle, alarmed to see Jack surrounded by two others he couldn't quite distinguish in the darkness. "It's OK, Ed. They're OK."

One of them started to talk and Eddie, though familiar with the lingo, pretended not to understand. "They had been discovered. Germans killed a couple of them but these two managed to escape somehow. Two or three days ago, from what I can gather. They've had no food or water, but I think they managed to salvage the reason for our missions, whatever that may be. I can barely understand a word they're saying."

One of the Frenchmen came forward beseechingly towards Eddie, talking non-stop and all of a sudden things were slotting into place and it pained him immensely to realise that he and his friend had been used as the same disposable fodder in exactly the same way as every other God-forsaken man that wore a uniform in an attempt to feel proud to do one's duty for one's country.

They were not considered human beings, nor would they be classed as heroes no matter the false promises of a shiny medal. Every mother's son that gave their lives over the past years would never know what little value they held.

Eddie had a sudden flashback memory of his father talking about being dismissed from his service as guard to his Queen, Victoria. He had no doubt about his father's loyalty and integrity so why he was sent away on grounds of ill health had always mystified him because his father was a picture of health and strength. Had it been another case of 'knowing too much' and getting rid of the evidence? Is that where he and Jack were now? Is that what happened to the other Frenchmen who weren't so lucky in their attempt to escape?

The larger of the two elderly Frenchmen continued talking whilst Eddie was trying to translate it in his mind.

"Jack," he eventually said. "We've been used as pawns. We've been delivering plans that these gentlemen were using to help make a new aircraft. We've been part of a massive relay team. I'm talking mega-massive! You've heard of Kawasaki, right?" Jack nodded, of course he had.

"Seems Rogers has, too. I can't even imagine where he fits into the equation, but you and I are helping the Japs build their new planes by passing on the plans that these guys have designed because they've been promised an absolute fortune. Their steam locomotives are already going far."

Jack stifled a laugh.

"And one of your Fenchies here, is the brother-in-law of the granddaughter of Mr. Kawasaki himself!"

Jack was even more confused. "But why here in France? Why this secret place, and to what purpose?"

Eddie reiterated a statement Rogers had used when he had raised questions months ago. "Ours is not to reason why, ours is just to do or die."

"So, we do or die?"

"No, we don't. We do and *live*, Kowalski. I don't want to try to understand it. The less I know the better. Let's go home. They'll have to stay here."

"But Ed, they're just a couple of old French guys. What you're suggesting is unbelievable. Even if we are passing plans backwards and forwards, how are they getting back to the Japanese?"

"By sea, my friend. Goodbye, Jack. See you back in Blighty."

Jack was totally bewildered as he watched Eddie jump on his bike and ride away. Looking at the confused faces of the two men he, too, was about to abandon, Jack felt such pity. He felt bitterly annoyed as well, because he knew - instantaneously - that Eddie had understood them.

"Eddie!" He called out after him, "Ed, wait! We can't just leave them here. They'll starve to death. Eddie, they'll starve to death…"

30: Evan, Now Aged 5

Evan's chitchat about his so-called past life never wavered. It was always about him being Eddie, his sister Meg, his old rival Jack, and numerous other accounts. He still had the occasional night terror but wouldn't remember anything about them in the morning, and whilst it was sometimes thrilling to hear him recount his memories, it was also disconcerting because he genuinely felt sad and missed these people once close to him, who were now long dead!

He was advanced for his years academically and mentally, yet still Sarah worried about him having no particular special friend to play with. It wasn't normal for a bright child to remain so isolated. Oh, all the teachers loved him because of his ability to cheer them up, understand a joke that the other children didn't, but she knew that when she was the same age, she had multiple friends.

"He'll come into his own when he's good and ready, Love," Bill would reassure her. "He has us and he's a happy enough chappie, content with his lot, I'd say." Which was meant to pacify but didn't.

Halloween was approaching and Sarah wondered about throwing a small party and suggesting Evan invite some of his school friends over. She could decorate the house with lots of skeletons, ghostly things, do some pumpkin carving, make toffee apples, hot dogs with fried onions. They could walk down their little cul-de-sac trick-or-treating at the neighbours' houses before eating. She'd make some invitations she could hand out to parents and was getting carried away with her ideas.

Asda did a great selection of Halloween costumes; she'd get one for Evan feeling sure he'd want a skeleton of some description. Some sparklers too; all kiddies loved sparklers. Bill thought it was a fabulous idea and insisted on making the hot dogs with fried onions.

"How about a big saucepanful of mushy peas, too, Sarah? Can't have hot dogs and fried onions without a hefty portion of mushy peas. Your mum used to make the best ones ever."

Sarah agreed, smiling at the memory of her mother stirring the big saucepan. A box of dried peas soaking overnight made a huge load.

"Do you remember when my friend, Jane Williams, kept going back for seconds? I think she had three or four bowls full of mushy peas with mint sauce and the next day at school, her mum told my mum off for letting her have so much because she never stopped farting all night."

Bill roared with laughing, "And Jane Williams wasn't on her own was she, our Sarah? What, with the fried onions and those peas, your mum was disgusted with you, too!"

Sarah, too, burst out laughing because that's a memory she certainly hadn't retained.

"OK, Dad, let's do it. We only live once, don't we?"

Bill raised his eyebrows then. "Ahh, well now, that's debatable isn't it?"

She made the invitations and handed them out to some of the mums of children she felt Evan would like to have at his party even though he hadn't suggested a single name. Sarah had developed a nice rapport with a few mums and decided to do the inviting herself, telling them that she would be providing a big bowl of punch for the adults.

"Can't let the children have all the fun can we, ladies? Besides… there'll be no school the next morning."

All six ladies accepted there and then, saying they would look forward to it.

Between them, Bill and Sarah did a fabulous job with the decorations. There were carved pumpkins with candles burning inside, some cobweb fibers hanging from the ceiling and lampshades. Bats, spiders, paper ghosts, all the cheap

Halloween paraphernalia one could buy from the supermarket without breaking the bank if they were never expected to be used again.

Each child turned up in their chosen fancy dress costumes eager to go door knocking in anticipation of getting lots of sweets. It was already dark and very cold, but the children didn't care because they were determined to have fun on this special night.

Bill had already cooked the hot dogs and onions and once everyone had finished the trick-or-treating parade, he could microwave everything. He was enjoying playing host to a gathering of young ladies and their offspring. He'd bought several packets of sparklers and decided to buy half a dozen small fireworks to finish off the night, making it even more memorable.

Sarah was acutely aware that whilst everyone appeared to be having a great time, Evan seemed uncharacteristically quiet. He hadn't even wanted to wear his skeleton costume which she purchased feeling sure he'd be thrilled. Deciding to half ignore his lack of enthusiasm she helped herself to another glass of punch determined she was going to!

All the other children loved the occasion, the food, the mushy peas and the wrapped toffee apples they were being allowed to take home with them. The three little girls and three little boys squealed with glee at their sparklers, writing their names in the air and watching the glow of letters. Sarah watched as Evan began to write his name with his own sparkler and sighed with relief with the saw the V appear after the E.

"Now for the grand finale to your night, young ladies and young gentlemen, a few fireworks to get you in the mood for bonfire night next week. You can all watch from the kitchen window while I go outside to light them. Would one of you kind ladies pour me a glass of that punch for when I come back inside, please?"

The children all gathered at the kitchen window and oohed and aahed as the first firework whizzed into the night sky, bursting into a shower of beautiful colours and shapes which cascaded back to earth like iridescent confetti. Bill was thoroughly enjoying himself and quickly lit the second then the third so there was a succession of wonderment for his audience to enjoy; however, the fourth brought a huge anti-climax to the whole party as when the product of the firework descended back to the ground, loud bangs followed which surprised not only the schoolchildren but Bill, too.

He was disappointed because he never liked the loud explosive ones since being a young lad himself and watching his poor Border Collie tremble with fear every 5th of November. The noise had terrified her to the point of wetting herself and scrambling for cover wherever she could. He always maintained the best part of her older years was becoming deaf when she could no longer hear them.

Suddenly, Evan screamed in such a high pitched wail that made everyone stop looking out of the window and turn their attention to their friend who had darted under the kitchen table with his hands covering his ears, yelling his lungs out.

"Get down everyone!" he was shouting, "get down, get down!"

Sarah was mortified and hurried under the table to comfort him. She wrapped him up her arms hushing him, reassuring him whilst worrying what their guests must be thinking. Did they think her son was mentally disturbed, attention-seeking, a mardy spoilsport?

Bill had heard the commotion and rushed indoors, anticipating finding one of the children injured? He didn't know what to think had happened and then he spotted Sarah underneath the kitchen table with her arms around Evan and her faced uplifted to him in desperation.

He wanted to weep as he watched his grandson sob and shake and felt such an idiot for buying the damned fireworks that were supposed to be a treat.

"Evan, Love," he tried his best sympathetic approach, "it's OK, they're just fireworks. It's finished now. I won't light anymore. You can come out now. They're all done."

"The grenades, Grandad. They're too loud. They hurt my ears and they kill people. I don't like the grenades. You know I don't like them."

Bill was now on his knees talking softly whilst the mothers and children stood watching, in shock. "They're only fireworks, Evan, they're not grenades. Didn't you see the lovely colours they made in the sky? They're for fun."

Evan pushed Sarah's arms away and crawled from under his hiding place, "Well, I'm not laughing because it's not funny, and neither is this stupid costume." He started to peel off the top, dragged it over his head and slung it on the floor in disgust, "And you shouldn't make me dress up as a dead person, either."

Everyone stood stock-still in total disbelief. The children stared in silence, not understanding what was going on after such a wonderful night.

Evan didn't hang around to hear anything else because he ran out of the kitchen and upstairs to his bedroom, slamming his door behind him.

You could hear a pin drop in the ensuing seconds, with no one knowing what to say but deciding the decent thing would be for everyone to gather their belongings and leave. Sarah had run upstairs after Evan. Bill tried to pass off the incident as humorously as he could as Evan having an off day, probably over tired, too much excitement and the mothers nodded affirmatively declaring it was late and time to go home, thanking him profusely for their hospitality and hopes that Evan will be fine and dandy in the morning.

They were all walking out the front door when one of the mothers hesitated. She pressed the button on her car key fob and told her daughter to get in the car. She turned to face Bill and put her hand on his arm.

"My nephew was exactly the same. Some years ago, when he was a little lad he would tell stories of when he was a young boy captured and taken away from his country of birth, stolen from his family. He was packed onto a boat with hundreds of others and he remembered the stench was overpowering.

He was lined up at a marketplace where he was bought by some rich lady who wore a long green dress and a bonnet. We didn't know where he heard the word 'bonnet' from."

Bill listened attentively, not knowing where the conversation was leading.

"He said the rich lady made him open his mouth so she could see inside and examine his teeth. She paid the man, who had already paid the man who brought him over on the boat, some money and then took him to the big house with lots of land and he had to pick flowers every day - he said they were like his mother's cotton balls she used for removing her make-up, with the others who had the same brown skin as he. Bill, my nephew is white, and he wasn't even four years old."

Bill shook his head despairingly and sighed deeply. *"It has to be real!"*

"My nephew's name is Jacob but he was adamant his name was Jabari. Where in God's name he got that name from, my sister hadn't a clue, so after months and months of Jacob telling these incredible stories, she started to take notes and then began doing some research.

She discovered the name Jabari means *brave one* in Swahili and Arabic. I could stand here all night and tell you lots more but you need to go check on your grandson and I need to get Kylie home, but I'm here for you both if you need my help. My sister did manage to get a lot of answers for her and for Jacob. You and Sarah need your own answers, likewise, so does that sweet little boy of yours."

Bill felt liberated, lightheaded, and relieved to know that Evan wasn't the only one. Yes, Sylvia had had her experiences, but this woman had given him an open door to learn a whole lot more.

"Evan says he was Eddie, before. He was a cycling champion."

"A cycling champion, hey?" she smiled warmly, "I wouldn't have expected anything less. Look," she said rummaging around in her handbag, "here's my card. It's my business card but call me and we can meet anytime you like to compare notes."

"I will," he promised, taking the card.

"And thank you again for a wonderful night."

As Bill closed the door behind her, he was left pondering a couple of things.

One, he felt an enormous amount of... well, expectation somehow. This woman, he looked at the card for her name,

Linda Muse, this Linda had made it all sound so normal. Evan wasn't the only one to have these recurring memories of having lived in the past.

Two, she looked a lot older than the other mothers who came tonight, and she obviously wasn't a stay-at-home mum because she had a business card, so was she something of a career woman?

And thirdly, she was very attractive!

31: The Next Day

It was Saturday morning, the morning after the night before and the three were gathered around the kitchen table having their normal weekend breakfast of scrambled eggs on toast. Bill was making coffee in the coffee maker he hated using because he much preferred the easier method of instant granules. Boil the kettle and pour into the cups, simple! Why folk wanted to complicate the simple and easy act of making a cup of coffee was beyond him. He'd seen racks and racks of little sachets, miniature containers, and jars of exotic foreign blends in the supermarkets that promised descriptions of oriental tastes from islands he'd never heard of and wondered if the coffee did actually come from these far off lands or just another advertising ploy for Joe Bloggs to part with his hard-earned money, foolish enough to believe the expensive coffee was any different to the one he'd been buying since the year dot! His ever-proud motto was 'don't try to fix what isn't broken'.

He looked around at the now limp pumpkins scorched black from the smoke of the candles, and the cobwebs intertwined with black plastic bats, and laughed. "Looks like a scene from The Munsters in here with all this tack." The sink was piled high in paper plates with remnants of half-eaten hot dogs, bowls of dried-up mushy peas with white plastic spoons stuck in the middle left by the gaggle of youngsters with no appreciation of the simplicity of such a delicacy.

"How's our champ today? OK, Evan?"

"Yes, thank you, Grandad," he replied, "I'm better now. The grenades made me remember being back there. You see..." he paused for a second, "sometimes it's nice to remember and sometimes it isn't, like yesterday. I don't like it then."

Bill poured himself and Sarah a cup of coffee. "If you want to tell us about it, we're here to listen but if it's too distressing for you, we understand."

Sarah placed the plates of scrambled eggs on toast in front of them and joined them at the table.

Evan explained, "Most of the time I do like to remember and want to tell you. I liked it when I was Eddie... just not the loud bangs. I got a medal because they said I was brave."

Bill was so delighted to hear this new piece of information, "You got a medal, Son? Wow! Well, only the very bravest of the brave are awarded medals."

Grenades? Medal? Was Eddie *in the war*?

"So, when you received your medal for your bravery, was it for something different to the medals you won for your cycling?"

Evan's face lit up, "I won lots of medals for cycling, Grandad, and trophies that Meg polished every weekend after church. She was my best sister."

Bill was trying to connect all the names of the people he'd mentioned, not forgetting the bombshell quote of his Grandma Pat receiving her Friday's penny pocket money from Bert! He'd never heard Pat mention anyone named Bert.

"And Bert? I remember you telling me that Bert would give your Grandma Pat some pocket money, a penny, did you say? That wouldn't have bought your Grandma Pat a lot, would it?"

"That was before she was Grandma Pat, silly-Billy! She was only little, like me, then. Mummy can I have some marmalade on my toast, please?"

Bill cleaned his plate up and poured himself another coffee, eager to continue the momentum of the conversation.

"Ah, I see! So, Grandma Pat was just a little girl who Bert gave a penny to, on a Friday, like I do for you?"

Evan was overjoyed that his grandad was seeing the clearer picture. "Yes!" He exclaimed enthusiastically, "exactly the same cos Bert was Grandma Pat's grandad!"

Oh, it was complicated all right! Bill was totally lost in a sea of names and Evan's memories that he spoke about with the utmost confidence as if everything was crystal clear. He thought back to a conversation he'd had with Linda Muse, Kylie's mother. Kylie, for goodness' sake! What possessed normal people to burden a child with a name that? At the Halloween party there'd been a bevy of invented names in order to appear hip and hardly one that he classed as normal, and certainly none that he would ever remember!

At least Sarah had had the gumption to give Evan a proper name. It meant *rock* in Hebrew. A shortened Greek version of Evangelos – *good messenger* - and Evander, meaning *good man*.

"Evan," Sarah intervened, "so if you were Eddie, who was Bert… to you?"

"Bert was my friend, Mummy."

"You mean, like Jack was your friend?"

Evan rolled his eyes as if in despair at having to clarify things over and over. "Jack was a rival." He stopped talking, weighing up his next words. "Jack was my rival but we were friends too. Bert was my special friend because Meg told me about him, before I went. She told me I would meet him and I did."

Even though Evan was way ahead of his tender years, he knew how to hold an adult conversation, but Sarah and Bill were having difficulty understanding everything he was saying.

Sarah queried, "So Meg - your sister- told you when your were Eddie that you would meet Bert?"

Evan nodded.

"Dad, set the camera up!" Sarah whispered. Bill leapt up out of his chair to do as she'd asked, hoping Evan wasn't going to be too curious. "Focus it on all of us," she instructed.

"Evan, what's the date today?" She asked nonchalantly.

"All Saints' Day," he answered without hesitation. "It's when all the good people are welcomed in Heaven and we have a big, big party for everyone."

"And what about the 'bad' people, Evan? Are they not invited to this wonderful party?"

"No, not until they've passed the test."

"What test Evan? What's the test they have to do?"

Bill was beginning to feel a tad uncomfortable with his daughter's direct and slightly forceful line of questioning.

"We all have to do the test before we're allowed to live in Heaven. It's just the way it is, Mummy. God made the rules before Jesus went there. The rules have never changed and if you don't accept them then you can't come and live in Heaven."

Sarah was listening and trying to digest everything he was saying. "So if I was to go to Heaven and I told God I wasn't going to accept his rules, would happen to me, my dead spirit, where would I go?"

Evan looked at her with so much confusion, "Then you'd have to wait a long time until he decides to listen to you again and you promise to accept the rules. But why would you not want to? Everyone does."

"But what are the rules though?"

"They're all different, for everyone."

Sarah and Bill opted not to push anymore, afraid that Evan might clam up and refuse to cooperate. They wanted to reassure him of their support and interest without delving too deep and thus cause him distress. It had been heartbreaking to witness him hiding under the table, reliving some horrifying memories.

They were collating a lot of information now, making notes, video clips. However, they still needed a lot more information to find out if indeed Eddie did exist and why Evan was so sure he was now him!

32: Jack Kowalski – Back in France

Jack wasn't as fortunate as Eddie. Never had been, never would be. He wasn't as cocky or as confident, for one thing. Eddie was fair-haired, handsome, and funny. Jack was slight, skinny really, whereas Eddie was tall and despite the meager rations they were served, managed to retain some of his muscular physique. Jack had no doubt his friend would be fighting off the ladies when the dreaded war was over and they were back to normal, whilst he wondered if he'd ever be fortunate enough to meet a lady and marry.

His dear mother would disagree, of course, but what mother wouldn't? He envied Eddie in many ways. He had siblings, he had an interesting job back on Civvy Street, and he'd always managed to pip him at the post on too many occasions. Jack was fast, he knew that, and vowed to one day claim the first prize.

There would be no more rendezvous, their duties done though neither of the men knowing the purpose. He couldn't understand Eddie's theory on the Kawasaki business, it didn't make any sense and now it never would.

He felt pity for the two Frenchmen they left behind but doubted they would starve. Neither had any means of transporting them anywhere as their bicycles only barely managed to seat them!

Would he ever see Eddie again? Perhaps not, because he knew they were moving away, and chances were neither of them would survive. It wouldn't be so devastating for Ed's mother. She had more children, but Jack was an only child and with his father already being dead, he worried constantly for his mother. Would she leave the United Kingdom and go back to her roots? With his aunt getting married and moving away, more than likely with a family of her own now, she would have no reason to stay if he lost his life out there in France.

He dismissed his negative thoughts. He would be going back. He would survive, and he would do his damnedest to make sure that cocky so-and-so ate his last bloody words. Jack shook his head, smiling at his newly found determination to picture a future away from the Hell-hole he was in because if he was to continue with his nightly prayers and positivity, surely all that energy wouldn't be ignored or refused by the higher powers above indefinitely. *He* had to answer some of them. It stood to reason *He* wasn't able to accommodate every single one otherwise there would be no winners and the world would continue to be at war for an eternity, but if all hope, dreams and ambitions are lost... then life has no purpose.

The rains felt more dismal than the ice-cold winters, somehow. The skies were bleak, grey, and relentless. The soldiers were constantly saturated, cold, and more miserable than ever. Foot rot was all too prevalent and drying out footwear was impossible. Everyone's saving grace was that the opposition was in exactly the same situation. No blood had been spilled for days as it was impossible to attack under the horrendous weather conditions. The horses fell in the mud and struggled to get back on all fours, some damaging themselves irreparably and would have to be left alone to suffer agonising deaths, their pitiful screeching tormenting those who'd nurtured the beasts. A bullet was too valuable to waste on a mere animal when it could be used to end the life of the enemy, though some with compassion would end up using their own bayonet.

There was one particular horse that was a favourite amongst the men, Armin - a name that loosely translated to *whole* or *universal*, according to its devastated Suffolk owner who had no option in surrendering it to the war effort, along with her twenty others. It had been a sad sad day at the equestrian centre when they'd come to commandeer all of their beloved horses. Armin was just eleven months old, not even a yearling, yet it mattered not to those with clipboards with tick-boxes to fill.

Armin was considered almost another human being, considering his unique personality and seemingly understanding of his predicament. Everybody adored him and it was impossible to walk by him without feeling the urge to stop by to caress him and talk with him. How many secrets the young Armin hid underneath his mane would never be known, and yet he was universal. He was universal in that the young horse responded to everyone, eager for human company, as if he had been human in a past life.

He would saunter to the medical section and nuzzle the injured. He enjoyed more than his fair share of sugar rations, biscuits, a crust of bread with a smidgen of jam, but whilst horses can go for days without any food, they cannot go for more than two or three days without water and so the favored horse quickly developed a taste for tea, which - fortunately - there was plenty of.

Jack had always been a little nervous around the horses. Their formidable size and strength intimidated him. He'd never had any pets and a horse was a huge animal, hence he never volunteered to feed any of them yet one of his most poignant memories of his war days - along with many, mostly unwanted - would have to be the day he made an unbreakable bond with Armin, the whole horse.

It was one afternoon after a short exchange between the two opposite sides. A comrade - Dylan - had fallen, taken a hit in the thigh and he'd fallen onto a line of barbed wire that had been partially covered in mud. His clothing snagged and the more he writhed in pain and tried to untangle himself, the more difficult everything became. Medics were all over the place with stretchers trying to reach the injured. Gunshots fired constantly and Jack crouched down. Hearing Dylan's cries, he crawled towards him and was sickened to see blood spilling into the mud; no matter how long he'd been in the war the sight of blood would always make him nauseous. He wondered how those medics coped every day having to fix up people, tend to wounds that they knew would ultimately become infected and then gangrene would take over.

It took ages to free Dylan from the barbs and then he knew he had to try to drag him away from the line of fire and lead him to safety, whilst at the same time protect himself. They were sitting ducks, easy pickings for a sharp-eyed sniper. And that's when Armin galloped over. That young, fearless, human-like horse stood by the two of them, pushing at Jack's shoulder, pushing him away! He couldn't understand what was happening until Armin lay down right next to Dylan, and threw his head in almost a circular motion as if wanting to tell him 'I'm here, put him on my back!'

Jack did. He grabbed his comrade and placed him on the horse's back, which took some doing. Armin then began to rise slowly, stumbling a little until he gained his footing. He was up, standing, and Jack laughed with relief. "Go, boy" Jack slapped him on his rear but Armin stood there waiting. "Go, take him back." Armin curled his lips back showing his perfect teeth and stamped his foot in the mud, pawing it against Jack's own foot, and then he did something amazing that made Jack want to weep. Armin knelt down again, in front of him, waiting to take them *both* back!

Suddenly, Jack understood. Dylan needed someone to hold him whilst they made their way back to the medical section, so he did what he felt the horse wanted him to do and ascended, holding on to his wounded colleague and the mane of this majestic beast who then galloped away at lightning speed only to fall just a few yards after, getting himself tangled in a whole mass of barbed wire, and displacing both of his charges.

The horse thrashed yet made no noise. Dylan was now unconscious. Jack prayed, feeling they were all doomed and this was how he was going to die. He knew he had to try to detangle the horse's legs from the barbed wire but the cuts were deep and he shuddered at his own pathetic squeamishness, knowing that he must buck up and be a man!

Miraculously he did manage to free Armin's fetlocks from the rusty wire, remount, and get back to safety.

Dylan's wound was serious, and it was the end of his war days. He would be going to a hospital and hopefully, home. Armin wasn't so lucky. Left untreated, his legs would become badly infected and an injured horse was a liability they couldn't afford. He would be shot, like so many of the thousands of disposable animals. At least the troops would eat well for a while.

However, Jack could not forget that look in his horse's eyes. He felt he'd seen into his soul, if that could be possible, but that's what he felt and he was damned if the animal who'd saved him and a fellow soldier was going to be shot like a coward! The horse was a hero, and no way he was going to allow it to happen, "Over my dead body," he told God in his prayers.

The next morning, he went over to check on Dylan who was sleeping, so he then went to take Armin a slice of bread and jam and a biscuit. Armin instantly raised his head when he saw Jack and eyed the food. His ankles were bloodied and swollen and there was also a large laceration on his hind quarters. An overwhelming feeling of love enveloped Jack and he knew in that moment he was determined he could never ever allow this animal to be killed. If that had to be, why weren't the wounded men just shot and be put out of their misery when injured?

He hurried back to the medical section to find a doctor. He needed to plead with them to save his saviour, but all the medical team were far too busy attending to the wounded and hadn't the time to listen to him. He waited, and waited, and waited until he caught sight of a young nurse attired in the only thing he recognised, her once pure white pinafore bearing the Red Cross across her chest, just going off duty.

"Please," he begged, "this horse is special, and I know I sound crazy because I don't even like horses, but this one is different, I'm imploring you. He saved Dylan, and me, he's... Well, if it wasn't for him, we wouldn't be here right now. Can't you fix him up? Go and have a look at his wounds; can he be stitched up and bandaged like the rest of the men in the infirmary? Could you just take a look at him, please? If you say he can't then I'll have to accept that and I'll volunteer to be his executioner, I owe him that, but..."

The young nurse looked at him with pity as she wiped her bloodstained hands on her already bloodied pinafore. "Solider," she began compassionately "have you not seen all our wounded? We're not veterinarians, we're doctors and nurses. We don't have the knowledge to treat horses. We have limited medical supplies as it is, let alone extend them to just an animal."

This was true, of course. Jack half-heartedly agreed with her, but Armin wasn't just an animal and deserved a chance at least, and it didn't stop him from breaking down in tears at the seeming futility of his plight, embarrassing him no end.

Her name was Cindy, and Cindy couldn't bear to see him so heartbroken over an animal so she promised him she would take a look and see what she could do, but reiterated they couldn't spare any essential supplies other than maybe washing of the wounds and dressings.

Fifteen minutes later, Cindy found Jack sitting beside the horse everyone adored, stroking his big, beautiful head as his huge nostrils flared outwards and back again. She knelt down beside Jack, putting a reassuring hand on his shoulder as she looked at the torn and bloodied fetlocks. She knew that if they weren't treated quickly, they'd definitely become infected and then there would be no hope for the young equine.

"I have some iodine and bandages. That's all we can spare, soldier, and if you tell a soul, I will deny all knowledge and declare you stole them, do I make myself clear?" Jack nodded.

"My name's Jack. He's Armin, it means *whole* or *universal*. Thank you, nurse, I'll take full responsibility, thank you."

Cindy cleaned the cuts with tepid water and disinfectant, applied iodine and bandages while the gentle horse lay there as a grateful patient. When she'd finished, Armin raised his head and rested it on her shoulder, causing them both to laugh out loud.

"Where you from, Private? I can't detect your accent?"

"Leicestershire," Jack answered still looking at the patient, "but my parents are Polish, so I guess I must've inherited some of my mother's dialect."

Cindy studied him, "Really? I would have never known you were from Leicestershire, I'm from Melton Mowbray, the place famous for its exceptionally delicious pork pies. God, how I long to have one. We have them every

Christmas. It's tradition in our household as my dad is the pastry maker, an expert I may say!"

Jack was aghast "I'm from Melton, we're practically neighbours!"

Cindy was also aghast, "Really? What's your name, perhaps we might know people."

"Jack. Jack Kowalski," he replied, "my mum is a seamstress –"

Cindy interrupted, "… and she makes wedding dresses. Oh, good Lord above, you're the Jack Kowalski, the cycling pro your mother never stops talking about? I cannot believe this! Your mother made my sister's wedding dress! It was absolutely stunning, everyone said so." Cindy was laughing and shaking her head in disbelief, "This is bizarre…"

She sat back, looking at him, studying him almost, "You're not at all how I imagined you to be."

Jack had no idea how to interpret her declaration, "I'm sorry," he apologised, "I can't imagine what she told you."

"She's a proud mother, too, and now I understand why. Jack, if I'm permitted to address you by your Christian name?" He nodded as Cindy continued, "then one good turn deserves another, and I promise I will do everything I can to help your horse. I will sleep with him tonight and nurse him with all the care I would minister to a fellow human being, I can't give any guarantees though."

For Jack, that was more than enough. He patted Armin on his head and left, feeling a buzz in the pit of his stomach that felt like butterflies swarming around. Talking to Cindy had been like a breath of fresh air amidst all the daily sickening terrors and horrors. She knew of him: he'd watched her face light up when speaking of and recalling his dear mother, what were the chances of that? Is fate such a believable thing?

That night, he slept like a baby.

33: Bill and Linda

Linda was in the ladies' toilets applying an extra application of Yves St. Laurent lipstick before meeting her next client, admiring her new expensive hairstyle in the mirror and not begrudging a penny of the £500 it cost her. There was a new product to market, and she needed to be sure it was something worthwhile to send to her consumers to gain the necessary positive feedback. To Linda, the results mattered not as she was going to be paid handsomely anyway. The client came to her for it to be passed along to consumers and she would gather all the comments, positive or negative, and lay it at their feet, or - in this case - bound dossiers spread around the boardroom table.

Her phone beeped as it did endlessly and she sighed theatrically contemplating whether or not to read it as time was ticking on and she needed to be focused for the all-important meeting, but her female curiosity decided to press 'view message' because the number wasn't one recognised in her phone, then smiled reading the simple text.

"Hi Linda. Any chance we could meet up for a coffee and a chat? If you have the time. Bill, Evan's grandad."

It wouldn't have mattered if he signed off 'Sarah's Dad' or 'Evan's grandad', or just plain 'Bill', Linda would have known who he was, and smirked smugly as she sprayed a little more Chanel No.5 behind her ears before walking out of the ladies' toilets and into the sunlit boardroom where the fat cats sat waiting for her to join them. She acknowledged everyone serenely, professionally, "Ladies and Gentlemen, welcome once again."

*   *   *   *   *

It was a rainy Saturday afternoon and Bill had dropped Sarah and Evan off in Leicester city centre to do some retail therapy. She'd wanted to go to the Highcross Shopping Centre to find some winter boots, and the outdoor market for fruit and veg. Bill had told her he was meeting up with Linda in Crusty's, to which Sarah raised her eyebrows in surprise. "Just a meeting regarding our little project," he winked at her, yet in truth he wasn't altogether convinced that was his sole purpose. He'd been widowed a long, long time and having a little drink with an attractive and eligible female wasn't being disrespectful to the memory of his late wife.

He arrived before her and found a table to the side next to the large window that enabled him to watch out for her. Her bright yellow umbrella with cats and dogs was very apt, he thought, considering the autumnal weather. She sat down opposite him and removed her damp coat as the waitress approached.

"I hope my choice of venue is OK, Bill? It's my favourite little cafe to have a glass of white wine and a chip buttie and the patrons that frequent this place are so diverse."

Bill looked around, nodding in agreement. There was an assortment of different people, ages, cultures. An elderly couple - most probably in their 80s, a grandmother, daughter, and a crying grandchild. A group of college students, a single guy with more tattoos and facial piercings than he'd ever seen in his life… He tore himself away to focus on his 'date.'

Date? Was it really a date? He could live in hope.

"Thank you for meeting me," he said sheepishly, "I hope I wasn't being too forward?"

"Forward?" she laughed, "I gave you my card in the hope you would use it. So, two chip butties and two glasses of wine?" He chuckled inwardly, wondering what the lads at work would have to say about that!

The conversation began easily with no uncomfortable pauses. Bill asked her questions and she answered. Likewise,

Linda probed and learned a lot about the man sat in front of her.

Kylie was adopted. Linda had divorced her husband after years of putting up with his immature infidelities. "I wanted a family and he didn't," she further explained, "so I set up my own company and once it was established sufficiently enough to be able to hand over the reins to a trusted colleague when the need arose, I decided to reconsider my options on motherhood. It's very difficult for a single mum to adopt in the UK now, so I did a lot of research about the possibilities of adoptions from overseas. You have no idea how many children there are in these orphanages waiting to become part of a loving family."

No, he didn't.

"Kylie was 18 months and was pretty messed up. She'd been starved, abused, neglected. I had a whole lot of love to give and when I saw her little face… Well, I booked a flight to Korea and two months later she came home with me.

"I can't tell you how wonderful that felt, but it wasn't at all plain sailing, mark my words, not at all. She couldn't walk or stand because she'd been kept in a crib for such a long time. She couldn't understand a word I said, either, so she had to learn a whole new language. Eating was traumatic for us both because she'd never had solid foods, only a bottle. Can you imagine that?"

Bill shook his head, remembering Evan's progress as a baby and his determination to walk, feed himself, refusing to wear his nappies because he used the potty by himself.

"Was she already Kylie, or did you choose her name?"

"One of the nurses had named her Kylie because..." Linda choked at the sadness surrounding her daughter's past. "She'd been left on a rubbish heap. She was probably six months old. Naked, covered with bruises, and... when she was discovered, she was found with a dog curled up next to her, keeping her safe. She was 'lucky', the nurse said. 'She should be so lucky, lucky, lucky, lucky'... so they named her Kylie, after the singer of the famous song. Believe me, I would have liked to have changed her name, but I wanted her to have a familiar word to recognise, even it was just her unfortunate name."

"That's an incredible story, Linda. Well done, you, for doing what you did. She is indeed a lucky young lady."

Linda smiled as she took a sip from her glass of wine. "I'm the lucky one, Bill. She's brought me so much joy I can't begin to tell you. She's made me complete, and I have not one single regret."

"Do you think she remembers? You know, anything about before?"

Linda shook her head, "Who knows what these children remember, Bill? They say the first two years are the formative years but I sincerely hope not. She's five now, though of course no one knows her actual date of birth, so the orphanage did a rough calculation, and we have two birthday celebrations for her. One from the official documentation and the second being her adoption date. Lucky again, hey?"

Bill roared with laughter. He was thoroughly enjoying being in this woman's company. "Another glass of wine?"

"Of course!"

They'd finished eating their chip butties, which were truly delicious! The butter dripped from the hot chips and he decided he would most definitely pay a return visit to Crusty's in the not too distant future. Now to get down to the other subject he was eager to discuss after hearing how she came to be a businesswoman and a single mother. He was becoming more and more in awe of her.

"Your nephew, Jacob, did you say? Can you tell me some more?"

"Yes," she answered, "but he's fourteen now and doesn't remember a single thing, which is kinda sad, don't you think, or is it good that he no longer has to endure the painful memories?"

Ah! That was a question and a half. He'd never considered Evan would forget talking about being someone else before he was himself.

"But didn't your sister show him everything she'd collected and researched about the stories he told?"

"Of course she did, but he just laughs about it and says he doesn't have any recollection at all. As they grow, their past memories fade. Evan's will too, that's why I recommend you do everything you can to find out who he used to be. Names, dates, events, everything. Jacob told a wealth of fascinating details.

"He was obviously a slave, stolen from his family and country to pick cotton along with many others, to make the white folk a lot of money. He talked of fellow slaves trying to escape, which was heartbreaking, Bill, because although Jacob claimed the lady of the establishment was kinder, the overseer of the said 'merchandise' wasn't, and he'd go off in search of the poor souls with dogs! Most didn't get far because they tried to escape at nighttime and had no idea where they were running to. The overseer, according to Jacob, set traps around the perimeter of the plantation and many were caught in those horrific contraptions.

"They'd be forced to walk back, even though they'd be bleeding profusely and sometimes, no doubt bones were broken, too. A sick slave unable to work was a liability and those rich folk wouldn't waste money getting them fit again. It was cheaper to replace them with another."

Bill was horrified. He'd seen films and read books about this, but here was a lady sitting in front of him telling him that her nephew had experienced the whole thing! It was sickening.

Linda continued, "Jabari, as my nephew claimed to be, was a fit young man and even though he knew what would happen to him if he decided to try to escape, considered he had to give it a go.

"He was homesick. He missed his family, Jacob told us. His family would be worried where he was. He said he had no idea how long he was on the boat other than he watched the daylight pour through the open hatch on twenty-four occasions. He watched young women taken away and brought back later after many had taken turns with them, those from above deck.

"People unknowingly bought pregnant girls at the markets and then had them disposed of once they realised the situation. The more fortunate ones who had kind owners and acknowledged they could produce a continuation of a workforce were the lucky ones, for a short period of time.

"Some owners decided to stop separating the young girls capable of reproducing and built larger accommodation to house them all, rather than segregating the sexes. It pleased the slaves and human nature being as it is... free labour was born!"

Linda's revelations made Bill cringe for being part of an inhumane society. It was despicable to any decent person alive today.

"And Jabari, Jacob? What happened?" Bill asked.

Linda smiled, reflecting "I always considered I had two wonderful nephews, Bill. Jacob, of course, because he was the son of my sister, and Jabari because of who he once was. I loved them both and so did my sister. After a heck of a lot of intense research my sister was able to confirm everything Jacob had told them and eventually managed to locate a great-granddaughter of Jabari. It's surreal, isn't it? Jacob inherited not only Jabari's memories but a whole family and they adored him. It was incredible for him, at that time, because he felt such a strong connection with his roots, but now - sadly - it's all in the past."

Wow, it was an incredible revelation and he knew without any shadow of further doubt he owed Evan the same and was going to do his utmost to ensure it happened like it did for Linda's nephew.

Time had gone so quickly that Bill suddenly panicked and looked at his phone to check the time, so engrossed were they both in their conversations. He was supposed to meet with up with Sarah at 4.00 p.m. at Burton's corner and help her with the shopping bags and it was now 4.15 p.m. He rose from his chair proffering his apologies to Linda and asking if they could meet again, soon.

She said "Of course, I'll call you," and he hoped she meant it. Burton's corner was less than a minute away from Crusty's cafe and he was there seconds before his daughter and grandson arrived which stupidly flooded him with relief but couldn't understand why he felt so guilty.

34: Later That Night...

"Dad, Evan's getting his jimjams on before he gets into bed, do you want a beer?"

Bill turned down the sound to the TV and contemplated her simple question. "Do you know what, our Sarah, I think I'll have a whisky and orange, please. I've not had one of those in ages."

Sarah was amused, "No, you haven't. That was Mum's favourite tipple too, wasn't it? Do you want any ice?"

"No, Love, just as it comes. I want to talk to you, after we've said night night to Evan."

Bill had been consumed with everything Linda had told him that afternoon and he couldn't stop thinking about her. He hoped she would call him again, as she'd said she would.

Evan had been read his story with no mention of anything to do with his past, and went happily to sleep.

Back downstairs, Bill picked up his tumbler of whisky and orange, still feeling quite uplifted about his afternoon in the company of a lovely lady. Grief doesn't have to last forever, he told himself, and everyone deserves a second chance, his own daughter included.

"What's on the box tonight then, Dad?" Sarah asked jovially as she sat in the adjacent chair, almost spilling her own glass of Gin and Tonic that was filled to the brim.

"Cheers, Love," they clinked glasses.

"You know I met with Linda Muse today, Kylie's Mum?"

Yes, Sarah knew that. Surprised, but hadn't pushed.

"She's a nice lady, Sarah, and she's told me some amazing stuff. Did you know Kylie, her daughter, was adopted?"

Sarah didn't because it hadn't ever been mentioned, but now hearing about it, she could believe it because it was obvious. She'd assumed Linda's partner had been Asian?

"And Linda has a nephew, like Evan. Been here before, and her sister researched everything. Everything Sarah, it's terrible what that young nephew of hers had to go through a second time."

"A second time? What do you mean, Dad?"

"I mean a second time. Once in his previous lifetime and then again as he was reborn into his second time exactly the same as our little boy upstairs. Evan says he was Eddie before, and he's already tried to tell us what it was like but you and me will never be able to fully comprehend what's it like for him to live in two different time dimensions. Firstly as a man and then as your child and it's our duty to help him understand and help him."

"But we have been listening and helping him, we're doing all we can..." Her voice wavered.

"We're not helping or doing enough. We've listened, recorded, made notes, but we need to be reactive now. Evan will eventually forget everything about being the Eddie he once was and that's tragic, considering the journey he had to make to come back to be with us. We shouldn't sweep it under the carpet as if he had never lived before because I believe he did. I said it from day one and I'll continue to say it for evermore, our lad was here before and by hook or by crook I'll prove it!"

Sarah giggled, "It seems to me Ms. Muse has been quite an influence on you?"

"Shift your backside, you sarcastic bitch and help me get those damned albums out of the attic you pestered me to get when Bob and Sylvia came over. Now, while his lordship is fast asleep."

35: 1918 - The End of the War

No wonder it had all been quiet. The defeated German armies were hungry and had been rebelling. The light at the end of the dark tunnel glimmered brightly for Eddie, Jack, Bert, and all the rest of the surviving soldiers, airmen, and sailors. Home was so close now.

Many debated calling it a victory though a victory it was in the eyes of the top dogs, those who didn't have to leave the comfort of their homes and families... Those who never had to shoot a rifle or use a bayonet or throw a grenade – or kill a man. Sleep would never be encumbered by nightmares in such households.

Soldiers' spirits lifted. Even the sick and wounded found an inner strength to consider they would be seeing their loved ones again after all. To have a bath, sleep in a bed under the warmth of an eiderdown, eat proper food around the dining table and listen to normal family chatter.

Four years! God had answered their prayers, at last.

Eddie, Jack, and Bert were now all twenty-one years old, their past birthdays had gone uncelebrated but their future ones were ahead of them and they would never have to go to war ever again.

Eddie and Bert sat on the beach at Dunkirk amongst the 300,000 British and French soldiers waiting for a vessel to accommodate them.

"I always preferred a little secluded spot on the beach, Bert, not a crowded one like this," Eddie joked, "though to be honest, this is by far the best beach I've been on. What about you?"

"Wouldn't know, never been to the seaside. Don't like the water, I have a fear of sharks. Another reason why I didn't join the navy."

Eddie roared with laughter. "You're kidding? There are no sharks here, and you've never had your feet in the water, or swam in the ocean?"

"Never, and that's not the ocean, it's the sea."

"Oh, come on you seaside-virgin, take your boots off, feel the sand between your toes, the salt water will do our feet the world of good. Last one in is a sissy."

Eddie removed his worn-out boots and socks and ran towards the water, laughing like a schoolboy to join the hundreds already there doing the same thing, leaving his pal behind.

Bert watched and took out his harmonica from his jacket pocket. He played a short tune to no one, thinking about where he would go once he was back on British soil. He wasn't welcome back home, he knew that. His dearly beloved family had made their feelings perfectly clear the last time he went on leave.

He wished he was more extroverted, like Eddie, who seemed to never put a foot wrong and gathered friends like rotting fruit gathered wasps, yet Eddie was nothing like a rotting piece of fruit. He was the cherry that sat atop the icing on a cake - of which everyone wanted a slice.

He stopped playing his harmonica and leaned back on his elbows, supported in the sand, watching grown men splashing about in the sea, laughing, squealing, forgetting all their dirty deeds, wondering if he would ever find a reason to laugh again.

Eddie ran back to him, panting and demanding Bert remove his damned boots and join him, so he did. Bert approached the sea's edge with great caution, looking further out, checking for sharks that were not there. The sand felt gritty, cold, strange.

"We used to go to Morecombe for our holidays and our Meg would race me to the sea where she would dive underwater and swim like a mermaid."

Meg again! His blasted sister was so perfect, according to her doting brother, he doubted her very poo wouldn't smell of roses! Eddie was lucky, he granted him that, his own sister - Ivy - had never even deemed to send a letter, not one.

Then he let the water wash over his filthy, stinking feet and he tipped his head back, closed his eyes to savour the moment. Once again, the maniac was right, it did feel good. He paddled a little further, whilst still keeping his eyes on the horizon. Men were swimming in the water, fully clothed, having fun. It was surreal.

And then horror upon horror, Bert watched as Eddie stripped to his underpants and performed the ritual of washing himself. He flipped his long blond hair backwards as he emerged from under the water and wiped the excess away from his face, revealing a huge and infectious grin. Bert couldn't contain himself any longer, and joined in.

It had felt wonderful, that cold salty water managed to wash away weeks and weeks' worth of foul body odour, lice, dead skin. It was like a baptism of sorts, invigorating, a renewal of the soul.

No one knew how long they would be on the Dunkirk beach but it didn't seem to matter anymore because at least the mass evacuation was taking place and the sight of sailing vessels, big and small, gave moments to cheer and rejoice, wallowing in the delirium of accepting it was over.

Soldiers bided their time, waiting patiently in turn to board any sea-worthy contraption to take them away, hugging and kissing those too old or too young to have taken part in the war effort but still braved all elements to come to rescue those not so lucky; to bring every hero back to Blighty.

Meanwhile, Jack, Cindy, and Armin were facing their own battle, a battle of separation which Jack felt acutely. His regiment were clearing out and had received orders to head north to Dunkirk where they'd been told a huge rescue mission was underway. Cindy would obviously have to go, along with the rest of the medical team and soldiers, but the horses would have to remain behind, and Jack was devastated.

He was utterly torn because his heart wanted to go with Cindy but his bond with Armin was just as sincere and he couldn't simply abandon the animal that had saved his life, no matter how much pleading Cindy had done.

During their clandestine meetings when ministering to the horse, the young couple had managed to fall in love without actually telling each other. They made plans to reunite after the war and Jack promised her nights of dancing, evenings at the theatre, and Saturday afternoon teas at Chequers, in Loughborough.

He knew he was going to propose to her and envisaged a happy-ever-after scenario but it also included Armin and for some unthinkable and unbeknown reason, he also knew it was going to be here, in France. He wasn't envisioning leaving.

He'd developed a yearning to learn more about his equine friends and was willing to save them all yet had no clue how he was to achieve such a mammoth task as he had no knowledge of that at all. He'd spent so many sleepless nights concocting plans as to how he was going to transform his previous life into one that included the breeding, showing, and even racing of horses.

As everyone and everything was packed up in readiness to go, Cindy and Jack hugged and kissed their last tumultuous goodbyes. Jack's heart was breaking but his mind was steadfast. He'd write to his mother and beg her to come over and join him, like he'd write to beg Cindy.

And then she did something totally unexpected… "I'm staying, too. I can't go and leave you both. I've invested too much to leave you behind. Will you have me?"

Jack was aghast. "No," he demanded firmly, "Cindy, you have to go home, your family need to see you, please, go home. We'll be fine. I'll write to you the minute I'm settled and then – "

"I'm staying with you! I want to stay with you, Jack. Let our dreams become a reality now that we have a new chance. Hey, we didn't plan this, seems it's our destiny and you can't deny destiny."

Jack was shaking his head, determined she should return to England with the rest of them, to her family but Cindy was equally determined, "I'm not going anywhere without you, so if I have to go, you will, too."

That night they slept together for the first time under the remnants of the medical section and didn't give a hoot about what the morning would bring.

36: Bill, Sarah, and the Photograph Albums

Sitting up in the dusty dark attic space trying to find the boxes of albums now seemed not such a good idea after all. Why did everyone shove things up into the roof space that was inaccessible 99% of anyone's time? The simple answer because it's out of sight, out of mind.

"I tell you, our Sarah, my next house is going to be a bungalow with no attic, no garage to store stuff that never sees the light of day. It's ridiculous the amount of junk we human-beings store. If I died, you'd be left with the unpleasant task of chucking it all in a skip. I blame your mother; she was the one who kept every single memory. She kept boxes and boxes of your grandparents' stuff she'd inherited, too. Oh, look here, an empty chocolate box! Throw it to the side and we'll burn it."

Bill was feeling exasperated and his sudden sarcasm showed it.

Sarah took the lid off the chocolate box and unfolded a piece of paper inside reading the words...

"First gift from my boyfriend, Bill. I saved him the chocolate Brazil cos he said he liked them. I ate the rest."

"Aww, Dad. Mum kept the chocolate box! How lovely is that?"

"Let me see that."

"Here's another little box, looks like a jewelry box. Oh, another note inside,"

"First bottle of perfume from Bill. I love it!'

"Did you buy Mum some perfume, Dad?"

He did, he remembered. It was whatever it said on the bottle, Dior or something, he couldn't recall the name other than it cost him almost a whole week's wages!

"Sarah, let me see the note."

Pat had squirreled away boxes of priceless memories, and he had had no idea. He sat in that attic space surrounded by his late wife's treasures and felt ashamed. He felt ashamed because he'd stuffed them away, out of sight, as if unworthy of being remembered again.

Sarah dragged a suitcase over. "What's in here dad? This looks like something from out of the Ark!" It was a small cream vanity case, the type most ladies had in the 60s for a weekend away, with two buckled straps on both sides. She undid them and opened the lid... There were old sepia photographs, certificates, birth certificates, medals, necklaces, lipstick and make-up containers, envelopes and postcards, a beautiful hand-embroidered handkerchief, a whole cacophony of historical memorabilia that neither Bill or Sarah had seen before.

"Let's take everything downstairs. We can look at them together."

Unsurprisingly, Evan was the first to grab hold of a photograph of Bill's sweetheart, Pat, showing them on their engagement party.

"Aw," he declared, "Grandma Pat was so beautiful today. There was an announcement in the newspaper."

And there was; he was right. Sarah found the little newspaper cutting announcing their engagement that tallied with the picture.

It was a bittersweet experience for the two adults to pick up bundles of photographs and look through them. Bill handed one to Sarah, "This is when we went blackberry picking down Donington-le-Heath; your mum was pregnant with you. Picked over four pounds of berries that day. Pat made jars of blackberry jam and then some blackberry vinegar cough medicine. I preferred it on my Yorkshire puddings." Sarah smiled, watching his face soften as he took a much-needed trip down Memory Lane.

"Ah, it's so nice to see all these photos again. And this one, look, it's you with Santa Claus. Co-op or Lewis's, I can't remember."

Evan was now going through the small cream vanity case and suddenly squealed with glee, "Grandad, Mum, look! This is us, our family! That's me, that's Meg, there's May, Rose, and my mum and Dad. That's me, Mum, me when I was Eddie!"

Sarah grabbed the old photograph from him and studied the non-smiling faces of a family from eras past. She turned it over and read out the names on the back. Eddie, May, Meg, Rose. Eddie was in a soldier's uniform. He looked dashing indeed. How did Evan know who the people were, she'd never seen the photo before?

"Aarrggh," he screamed again much louder, "my medal from the war! I told you, Mum! Look, I told you!"

Again, Sarah grabbed it and looked at it earnestly, turning it over to find the inscription on the back but there wasn't one.

"It's on the rim, Mum."

And it was all there. The recipient's name, Edward Tyler, his rank, and unit, and Sarah wanted to weep. She passed it gently over to Bill who was equally dumbfounded.

"And wow, look Grandad, this is me and Jack Kowalski when we met up again after the war and here's my mum and dad on their wedding day! Why aren't they smiling?"

Evan was beyond himself with excitement as he rummaged through the little case, bringing out more and more of his past. It was mind-blowing.

"Meg and Bert with Grandma Pat as a baby, May and Will. Rose... Oh, poor Rose."

"Evan? Meg and Bert with Grandma Pat? *Your* Grandma Pat?" Sarah asked intrepidly. Evan nodded so happily, thrilled to see he was being believed.

"But how do you know these people in the photos, Evan, you weren't even born when these people were alive. I don't even know who they all are or why all of this stuff is in our attic."

Evan shrugged his shoulders, "Grandma Pat must have kept everything, I suppose. I'm glad she did. Perhaps she left them for me to find."

"I know why it's all in the attic, Love. Your mum kept everything didn't she? The first tooth you lost, the little wristband the hospital provided when you were born, the boxes of the gifts I bought her... Good grief, I had no idea she was such a silly sentimentalist... But bless you, my dearest wife," he said looking up to the ceiling, "I'm so glad you were."

Next came the birth certificates, marriage certificates, the wedding bans of Eddie's parents.

"Mum's grandparents, or great-grandparents I haven't done the maths yet, seem to have been married in the chapel at The Tower of London! Surely that can't have been possible, Dad?

Evan butted in, "Mum and Dad had special permission from the Queen because she liked him. I told you before, Grandad, he had a jacket and hat like the tin soldier in the story book."

"Your name was Edward Tyler, Evan? Before, I mean..." Sarah pushed.

"Yes," he answered immediately, "but everyone called me Eddie. Meg was Margaret but she was Meg, really. Johnny died... But he's OK now. I didn't get to know Johnny."

"Dad," Sarah turned to Bill, "we have surnames, and with all of this… stuff here of mum's, we have something to go on, haven't we?"

There was one question neither Bill or Sarah dared to ask, feeling it might tip Evan over the edge. They had an abundance of information spread out on the living room carpet but nothing about his death and Sarah was afraid he would eventually find his own death certification in the little case amongst the heap of papers and photographs.

Before she could move the case away and try to steer him towards the more recent pictures of her own younger days, Evan held up another photograph and suddenly his excitement waned, his face sombre, "This day was the best day of my whole life."

Sarah leaned over to take a closer look at the picture. There was a grinning Eddie on a bicycle with one arm over another man of smaller stature, grinning equally. "Me and Jack," he explained, "Tour de France. He was fast, Mum, really fast, but not as fast as me."

*   *   *   *   *

Bill had been contemplating taking early retirement for a while now, especially as Evan was growing up and he felt he'd already missed a lot of his formative years. Even though he knew he wasn't Evan's dad - for goodness sake, according to Evan he'd already had two fathers! - but he was the only father figure in *this* life he would have!

Bill also secretly hoped he would have more of a relationship with the lovely Linda Muse, and was watching his phone like a love-sick teenager waiting for her to message him to arrange another meeting. Playing hard to get, no doubt, but at his age, he felt game-playing was old hat. Anyway, he never did understand the way women's minds worked, his recent discovery in the attic was testament to that!

The following Monday morning he approached the personnel department to discuss his retirement plans. He wanted to know how much notice he needed to give and ask about his pension benefits. In actual fact, money wasn't the deciding factor in any shape or form because the insurance company paid out after Pat's accident to the princely sum of £250K.

He was considering purchasing one of those nice log cabins in Wales where he and his little family could spend summers, bank holidays, long weekends any time they liked. Perhaps even - if he was to think and hope long-term, Linda and little Kylie too?

The other miners envied his ability to consider jacking it all in and living off what was in his bank account, hardly considering the heartache behind the accumulation of such funds.

Sitting in the canteen after a normal shift, downing their bacon butties with brown sauce and mugs of strong sickly-sweet tea, Brad Wilson wanted to add his unvalued and unsavory opinion from a neighbouring table. "You don't know how lucky you are, Mate! A rich widower and no more trouble and strife to boss you about anymore, I say go for it. Enjoy yourself while you still can."

Bill cringed, deciding to ignore the idiot. Jimmy, sitting opposite Bill, rolled his eyes, "Ignore him, Bill. I'm sure his wife wishes the same for her. Anyway, you were saying... you had a date? Wow, must say I'm surprised, but also... good for you! I hope it works out."

Bill was quick to reassure him, "Well, it wasn't an actual 'date', as such. I just met with her because we had some things to discuss. We have something in common, see."

Jimmy slurped his tea whilst listening.

"Her name's Linda Muse, and she has this daughter who's at the same school as Evan. They came to our Halloween party, and she had a very interesting story to tell about her nephew which was not dissimilar to that of our lad."

Jimmy stopped drinking his tea and leaned backwards, staring at Bill. "Linda Muse? Not *the* Loony Linda Muse?"

Bill was confused, "Loony Linda? I'm not following you."

Jimmy moved forward, "Loony Linda doesn't have a daughter, Bill. She was married to a real great bloke, but she was putting it about everywhere, man. The butcher, the baker, the candlestick maker. She is a very sexy woman, I'll grant you that, and her poor old man was ridiculed. Made to look like a right fool."

Bill was mortified. "That can't be true, Jim. I've met her daughter, she told me the story of how she adopted her from Korea and – "

Jimmy interrupted, "Young Kylie? She's her next-door neighbour's girl. Linda takes her to school every day because Jeab, the mother, works at the hospital. Didn't you know?"

Bill was totally confused, "But she told me about her sister's boy and his –"

"Linda doesn't have a sister, nor a brother. She is a very cunning and unscrupulous businesswoman. Please don't tell me you've promised her any money!"

Bill collected his thoughts. No, he hadn't promised any money because such conversations hadn't arisen. He couldn't believe what his colleague was telling him. It couldn't be true. But Jeab? That sounded like a foreign enough name, oriental even?

Jimmy felt awkward and so sorry as he watched his friend's face melt into a worried expression, "Aw, Mate. I'm sorry, I just don't want you to be taken for a fool, and you won't be the first. She's a clever woman. Fooled her husband sure enough, and he was the one taken to the cleaners because she even paid some geezer to knock her about a bit and blamed it on the hubs. And mud sticks. He lost his job, his home, his reputation. Lives in Oz now. Met up with an ex-girlfriend on Facebook and is living the dream with his wife and two sons."

Bill did feel foolish and couldn't speak. "Delete her number, Mate. You deserve better than that."

He left the canteen in a fog of numbness and disbelief. Everything she'd told him about Jacob / Jabari, had been total fabrication? It couldn't be so, she'd told the story with so much conviction, and to what purpose would anyone want to invent such a story? She was so convincing; how could he possibly not believe her? It didn't make any sense.

Driving home, his thoughts were filled with Linda Muse, the woman he'd had fun with that wet, rainy Saturday afternoon in Crusty's, enjoying the simplicity of chip butties and white wine with a nice young lady. His bubble well and truly burst. "Aw, Pat," he said out loud, as he often did when driving alone, "why did you leave us? Why couldn't you have waited until we were old, like we planned?"

He wiped his tears away in order to watch the traffic lights change. "I wouldn't have done that to you, wouldn't have let you suffer like I've... You missed out on your grandson. You missed out on meeting your uncle, I believe he is. His name is Edward, Eddie as Evan says he is, was. He's a grand lad, Pat, you'd love him, as we do, Sarah and me.

"I'm sorry if you feel betrayed because I enjoyed the short company of another woman, but... ah, well, I guess I'm just an old fool after all. Talking of old fools, you even kept the box from those chocolates and the perfume box? What was that damned perfume? Dior something? Miss Dior? It was, wasn't it? You will have no idea what it meant to me to find you'd kept those memories. It was good for our Sarah, too, because she was able to realise now, as a mother herself, how much we loved each other. And we did, didn't we?"

BEEEEEPPPPP! Bill looked into his rear view mirror and then ahead as the traffic lights changed to green, and pushed the gear stick into first then second, waving an apology to the impatient driver behind, wondering why everyone was in such a hurry to race on, his reverie totally bastardised.

By the time Sarah and Evan walked in after school, they were surprised to see Bill still sitting propped up against the settee in the living room, going through the heaps of old photographs. For most of her life, Sarah could only remember it being her and her dad. He'd been her rock, her everything. Memories of her mother were vague, which saddened her but then she had Miles and eventually Evan.

Of course, all her memories and photographs were stored on Facebook, iCloud. Nice to view from time to time, but there is nothing to compare with having an actual piece of glossy paper in your hands that's a piece of history, like the unseen-before picture of her ancestors. Her own little boy from a past life which she tried to see any resemblance but couldn't.

They now had Eddie's war medal, with his surname, rank and unit. They had photographs, certificates, and they had the blissful searching tool to find out everything - the internet.

Sarah had become adamant she was going to include Evan in all of their research from now on. It was for him, after all.

The laptop was set up and Evan sat between his mother and grandfather as Sarah typed in 'Edward Tyler'. So many hits that suggested numerous Edwards, Eddies, Eds, etc., etc., etc.

They each looked to each other in despair.

She continued typing *Eddie Tyler and Jack Kowalski*, Suddenly Evan jumped up and down like he'd just found out he had the winning lottery ticket to the umpteen millions when a black and white picture appeared on her screen of a similar picture of Eddie and Jack she'd seen amongst her mother's keepsakes.

"That's us, Mum. That's me and Jack in France. Look at me Mum, look, it's me when I won, but Meg was sad and cried afterwards. She told me she would wear our mother's black coat. I tried to tell her not to cry but then our mum came out and said 'Meg, who are you talking to?' and

Mother chastised her for talking to herself, but she didn't really talk to herself cos she was talking to me."

Evan was coming out with words he couldn't have known. Chastised?

"Meg had come home from Manchester, it was a holiday. She was scrubbing the back yard step and I wanted to hug her, to tell her I was sorry, and that I'll miss her, she didn't really see me, but she knew I was there."

Bill and Sarah sat in silence to let Evan continue telling his story. "I had to let her know first, but she knew anyway. She always knew, Meg was special that way, she should've been in charge, but they didn't let ladies be in charge…"

Sarah eased her way slowly into the conversation, pointing at the image on her laptop screen, "So that is you, Evan? You and your friend, Jack Kowalski?"

"Yes," he said, nonchalantly, "and then I died."

37: Tour de France, 1920

Eddie was renting a small one-bedroomed cottage in Osbaston, rather than go back to living under his parents' roof and Bert took lodgings in Heather to be closer to Meg, now that they were courting, having found out that his friend was correct on all counts with regards to his sister. It was the happiest Bert had been in years!

Normality was returning in the UK. Eddie went back to his former position as journalist and Bert got a job at the brick and tile works in Ellistown, not too far away. Building materials were a necessary commodity and fortunately England now had her men back to build again, enabling the women who had been working there during the war years to keep the factories going, to return to being mothers and housewives.

Eddie had received a letter from Jack informing him of his decision to remain in France where he and Cindy were now running an equestrian centre, having rescued several war horses from the impending trip to the abattoir. They had married and were expecting their first child. Life, Jack wrote, couldn't be better.

The two pals of older days corresponded regularly about their plans to participate in the fourteenth edition of the Tour de France and Eddie cycled every day to everywhere in preparation. He'd been invited to stay with Jack and Cindy and Eddie was beyond excited, not only to meet up again and chew the cud, but to take part in one of the most prestigious and arduous cycling events ever. It wasn't just a case of speed this time, but also endurance and only the fittest would last the course of over five and half thousand kilometers. This undertaking was a totally different ballgame to the contests they'd previously entertained because the route would take several days to accomplish.

Practicing this adequately for both men was nigh on impossible due to their commitments, their jobs and lifestyle. Eddie would use his weekends and cycle to Wales or Skegness, camping overnight then travelling back. Jack couldn't do anything like that because he had horses to feed and a pregnant wife to look after, so he physically trained with weights, logging, etc, and whilst they wanted to win, they felt their chances limited but at least it would give them knowledge and experience for the following year.

Eddie had to take a whole month off from work as the event took over twenty days to complete. He packed a small haversack, withdrew his entrance fee money from the building society and made his journey to Dover where he would take the ferry to Calais. Jack had given him instructions to head for Dunkirk, where they would rendezvous and take him back to Jack's home. It felt odd, the very thought of returning to Dunkirk, but Jack lived about ten kilometers away now, so all would be different.

It was a hot June day in Calais when he disembarked and the breeze from the English Channel was a blessing. The heat, he suddenly considered. Boy, he hadn't taken the weather into consideration.

Their reunion was an emotional one, with both men smiling from ear to ear and hugging like a couple of lovesick homosexuals, slapping each other on the back and breaking apart took more than a few seconds. "Good to see you again, Jack/Ed," they said as one. "Still as ugly as ever, Ed. That why you're still single?"

Eddie howled, "In your dreams, Kowalski, I'm still fighting the ladies off, as well you know."

They talked non-stop in Jack's pick-up where Eddie's bike and haversack lay in the back. They talked of England and how she was recuperating after the bombings, properties and roads being restored, extended, redeveloped.

Antonia, Jack's mother, had been to visit several times and was thrilled to know she was going to become a grandmother, hoping to be blessed with a granddaughter so that she could make some pretty dresses at last. Mary had a son, so she couldn't indulge her passion there. She was considering moving to France to be closer to her family but was concerned about becoming a burden to her son and new daughter-in-law so, for now, she was biding her time. Besides, Jochen hadn't survived the war and Mary was a young widow, finding herself in exactly the same predicament as Antonia was herself once upon a time.

Eddie took a huge breath upon arriving at Jack's home, envying the beautiful expanse of space, trees, the horses thundering round and round the huge paddock or simply grazing without a care in the world. The cottage was picturesque with climbing roses around the entrance, managing to intertwine with the louvred panels of the wooden window shutters. Chickens scuttled up to them, squawking with excitement which had Cindy rushing outside, wiping her dainty hands on an embroidered pinafore which shyly showed her expanding tummy and Eddie could instantly see what had made his friend chose this delightful, beautiful woman for his wife. Jack was far from a giant of a man and his wife was so petite they complimented each other perfectly but he'd never seen a more beautiful woman, her rich auburn hair was tied back into a ponytail, and she had this almost bronzed glow about her. Her green eyes seemed to sparkle when she looked at Eddie and hugged him into a sincere welcoming embrace. She took his breath away!

Her smile never left her perfect face and Eddie wanted to turn to face his friend yet was unable to take his eyes off Cindy, "You are the luckiest man on this damned planet, Kowalski, and I hate you!"

Jack grinned, feeling truly conceited to have that oneupmanship on the friend *he'd* always envied!

After Jack was shown his bedroom, which again oozed charm created by a woman's femininity, yet he knew he would enjoy a good night's sleep, he was offered a bath, a tour of the property and a chance to meet the horses, all before sitting down to eat dinner.

Eddie found himself nodding like a jealous fool, acknowledging everything he was shown, realising Jack was definitely the overall winner. He had the perfect wife, the ideal home, the ultimate prize: completion.

They leaned against the wooden paddock fence watching the horses. Armin was no longer a young colt. He was a superb specimen, a majestic stallion and came trotting over to greet them. "This is my reason for everything you see here, Ed. This boy saved my life and gave me a life I could never have imagined. I think perhaps we saved each other, didn't we, Armin?"

Armin neighed loudly, tossing his head up and down as if confirming Jack's statement. "I was terrified of horses before... but then I met this brave amazing fella, and now... well, no amount of money on this earth could ever part me from him. He's priceless."

Armin galloped away to join the rest of the herd now that the introductions were over. Eddie nodded, his brow furrowed in envy.

The morning sun shone brightly through the open window of Eddie's bedroom, and he was already throwing back the sheets as the smell of toast drifted upwards. He walked to the window to look outside and debated what idiotic part of him hadn't followed his friend's footsteps and remained in France to build a new life? It wasn't as though he was abandoning his roots, for goodness' sake; his own family was part French! He'd even suggested he and Meg return to trace their other family members; why wait? Look at what Jack had achieved. He could easily forsake his rented cottage back in Osbaston and have the guts to do what young Jack had done: make a life, a *real* life, one worth living.

He went downstairs to find Cindy alone at the table but - being six months pregnant - took to holding herself as she clumsily arose from the table to make Eddie a pot of coffee, explaining that Jack had gone to go the henhouse to collect eggs.

"He's so happy to have you here, Eddie, we both are. I've heard so much about you."

"Regrettably, I heard little about you," he answered truthfully, "until his letters came."

Cindy smiled, still caressing her unborn child, "He's envious of you, you - being the better cyclist and all. He's always wanted to emulate you."

Eddie guffawed, "Jack's envious of *me*? I'm envious of *him*! Hey, I may have been the fastest cyclist back then but he's definitely become the better achiever of us and... and I'm in awe, totally in awe of what he's... what he has and what he's done. I love the guy, but Cindy, would you understand if I admitted that I hate the man, too?"

Cindy was laughing out loud when Jack walked back inside with a bowl of freshly-laid eggs from their chickens.

"Your friend has just told me he makes the best scrambled eggs," Cindy teased, "so I told him to go ahead and prove it. You and I will sit outside and let him cook in peace."

With four days until the start of the Tour de France, they had time to practice before traveling to Paris to join the rest of the competitors. Even just a day of indulgence meant a heck of a lot of extra catching up to compensate, which was non-stop pushing, exercise, checking their bicycles to ensure they were in tiptop condition. No chance of neglect or failure to dismiss all they'd invested. This was their grand reunion, their own personal fight for notoriety and - friendship aside - they were going to battle on non-British soil.

Jack drove his pick-up truck with both their bicycles and luggage lying together in the back and conversations were stilted as both men tried to imagine the challenge ahead. Paris was heaving with traffic which wasn't unusual but now there was even more with radio crews, supporters, competitors and their entourage and Jack hadn't anticipated where to park, or enroll, or even finding accommodation.

Eventually they parked up the truck on the outskirts of Paris and cycled together to find out all the necessary information, dismayed to find themselves at the end of a long line waiting to collect their numbers, maps, and instructions.

"I am not paying some ridiculous price to have a bed for the night, Jack. I suggest we sleep under the stars as we did before, it's warm enough at least. Shall we have a celebratory glass of red wine or a beer before we do this?"

It would have almost been a comical sight to see the two men walk down the Champs-Élysées stopping at a cafe for the simple reason of enjoying a quiet drink in each other's company. One tall, blond and muscular; his partner, short and lithe, but too much was at stake to worry about what other folk were thinking. A coffee and a croissant were going to have to be enough… And it was enough, and had been enough for them, but there will always be an unexpected audience in the crowds, a forgotten face. Some people who, no matter the years and the history under the bridge, will never forget and hold tight to a grudge for evermore.

138 competitors lined up side by side, front to back. Eddie was number 137 wearing a white vest top and Jack 138, in yellow. A starting pistol was fired, and Eddie saw Jack stiffen for a split second, "Leave it Jack," he mentally urged, "go, go, go!"

It was a magnificent sight as all cyclists sped off amidst the deafening cheers of encouragement from the spectators lining the streets, and an exhilarating moment for the two Englishmen.

The first stage was completed by them both without any duress. They hoped to continue as successfully over the next ones or at least qualify for a share out of the prize money. Many cyclists would have cause to drop out along the way due to injuries, fatigue, or bicycle failure. It would also be beneficial for the weather to be in their favour, not too hot and not too wet.

Jack had been among the first twenty to arrive, which gave him a great feeling of accomplishment, Eddie followed shortly afterwards, and every other cyclist had done likewise. Having the first day and only 182 kilometers behind them, they were beginning to wonder what they'd let themselves in for.

"We knew it wasn't going to be a walk in the park, Ed. Three weeks, five thousand kilometers, mountainous territory and twenty-nine degrees of heat isn't for the faint-hearted but remember… we survived four years in mud and then the soaring temperatures of the summers, blood and guts, no decent food, with exactly the same yearning to reach the finishing line. We can do this again."

Eddie agreed. "Of course, we can and we will do, and when I get the prize money from my winnings I think I'm going buy a little place like you've done and become your dreaded neighbour. I already speak a little of the lingo so the transition shouldn't be that difficult for me. Despite being in France during the war years, Jack, I always considered it a beautiful country and often thought about returning to try to find some of my mother's family."

Jack laughed at his assumption he was going to win and also the prize money was going to be to buy a property. "You seem to have forgotten the prize money isn't for the one who finishes first, it's split between all those who complete, and as for you being a neighbour... Well, promise me you won't buy anything too close."

Week one - completed. Week two - completed. The third week was unbelievably exhausting, but the camaraderie and support of every competitor was far from exhaustive and the two friends were proud to be up there amongst the top twenty.

"You and I should be able to move up a notch or two over the next stages, Ed. Look here," he said pointing to the map, "let's forget about stage 11 for the time being, that's the toughest for everyone, but our bikes are lightweight, at least lighter than the others I've seen, and coming back down here, see…" again he pointed on the map, "you and I will fly down here. We should own this stage and it will elevate us further up the ladder. If we do, we should be placed in the first ten."

Eddie studied the map and grinned widely. "Jesus, Jack, it would! I hardly dare consider it, but I agree with you… but then stage 11 looks incredibly tough."

"This is the infamous Tour de France, Eddie Tyler, not some Sunday afternoon leisurely bike ride around Bradgate Park!"

38: Bill, Present Day

Bill hadn't deleted Linda's number. He couldn't bring himself to because he was in two minds whether or not he wanted her to call him again. She hadn't, and he felt a tad disappointed because he couldn't believe the story his friend had told him. Granted, he was much older than her but isn't age just a number? They'd enjoyed a lovely afternoon and he'd been looking forward to the chance of meeting her again despite the gossip, and gossip it must have surely been?

He'd actually tried to find out information on Jabari to see if anything could adhere to her supposed nephew's past life but was unsuccessful, and Sarah said she couldn't categorically confirm Linda was Kylie's mum, only that she took her to school every day and had assumed she was the mother. So, Bill threw himself into putting his retirement plans into action and buying a holiday log cabin in Wales, deciding Evan should be making memories as Evan, with Sarah as his mother and he as his grandad in this life!

Since the last weekend spent looking through the photograph albums and family historical documents Pat had saved and the internet searches trying to find Edward Tyler and Jack Kowalski, everything young Evan had told them was proving, so far, to be more than likely true!

Bill remembered the time he'd taken Evan to Hugglescote Park to ride the new bike he'd been given for his birthday and Evan suggesting he visit the grave of his Grandma Pat and 'him before,' which Bill hadn't understood, yet now he began to question and analyse Evan's meaning.

Was Eddie in fact buried in Hugglescote Cemetery? But he'd said he died in France? He returned from the war, they'd clarified that because they'd found rental papers appertaining to a cottage he'd rented in Osbaston, so he definitely didn't die as a soldier.

Evan had talked of going back to France to take part in the Tour de France along with Jack Kowalski, *"the best day of my life"* he exclaimed when Sarah showed him her laptop screen and he'd been soooo excited to see himself and the friend he never forgot.

"Is it real?" Bill asked himself for the umpteenth time. "Do we get second chances to come back again, and if we do, why? Why did Evan have clear and precise memories of his life before, when not everyone else did?"

Linda had been most clear about recording everything because her nephew eventually forgot when he reached a certain age. Now, was that real or was that made up for effect? 'Loony Linda' Jim had called her. What if she wasn't loony at all and she was recalling her own past memories? If he didn't ask her the burning question himself, he'd never know!

Linda was sitting at her PC typing a generic memo to a dozen of her clients when her phone beeped. She glanced at caller ID and smiled; it was Bill. She'd been anticipating the call.

She had liked the man and had a pleasant encounter killing an hour or two in his company whilst she waited for her nail appointment. He was a nice enough bloke, easy to manipulate, cast a line and reel him in, garner the sympathy vote about the adopted daughter et al. Well, she *felt* like the girl's mother anyway, ferrying her backwards and forwards to school like her own mother should be doing! These so-called career women expect everyone else to do their duty at the drop of a hat! Linda was also a career woman but took the time to ensure her sweet little girl next door arrived at school safely and on time and went to parties.

Little white lies never hurt anyone. She hadn't lied about Jabari because that was all true enough, only that it was her own past life and not that of a nephew. So what? It was a defense mechanism; she needed to protect herself as much as Jabari had tried to protect himself.

Bill had asked the ultimate question, which she'd successfully managed to avoid answering, "What happened to him?"

Linda hated dogs. As a child she'd always feared them, especially the big ones, the menacing ones with big teeth that smelled of blood like that of her neighbour's from years ago that would come bounding up to her with a ball in her mouth, expecting her to throw it in play. She despised that animal with her ridiculous pink fluffy ball, expecting to be forgiven!

The teenage Linda, however, wanted revenge. She knew her father kept antifreeze in the garage in readiness for the winter months and was of an age to know what antifreeze given to an animal would do.

As Jabari ran and ran trying to find his way back to his beautiful country and family, panting and wheezing while the dogs barked and snarled, snapped and tore at him as he fled through the terrain filled with traps, he eventually succumbed and fell to his knees, screaming in agony as he tried to prise the contraption open. Not minutes later the rest of the pack arrived, and the overseer watched sadistically as the dogs - in a muffled silence, save for Jabari's horrific screams - devoured him.

It was now her turn to sit back and watch sweet revenge take place.

She smiled smugly as she deleted the text message and number from her phone. She hated the name 'Bill' anyway: William Farrel was the overseer at the nice lady's plantation, but all those incarcerated lived in perpetual fear because of one particular evil, inhumane bastard, Bill. Bill Farrel.

*   *   *   *   *

"Sarah, I have something I'd like to talk to you about... my plans for my retirement and our future."

"Our future? You're not thinking about making a will, are you? Are you ill? Is something wrong Dad? Tell me now!"

Bill shook his head reassuringly, "No, Love, I'm fine, honestly. It's just that I've been thinking recently... you know, about afterwards. It's important to have these discussions now and make arrangements because one never knows what's around the corner. Take your mum's accident for example. We never anticipated that in a million years, but it happened just the same as billions of other such accidents happen and I want to make sure you're both secure, financially at least. Hmm, that's what I'm trying to say. I've been in touch with my pension companies and made arrangements for all my benefits to be paid into your bank account. I've given the personnel department at work my notice to leave at the end of next month and I want us to go and have a look at a log cabin I fancy down in Wales. What do you think?"

Sarah, though initially somewhat speechless, was thrilled. "What do I think? I think it's a fabulous idea, Dad. Mum would be pretty chuffed to know you're actually getting around to spending the money from the insurance company at last *and* taking early retirement! But… what's brought this on all of a sudden?"

"Well," Bill began, "I want our boy to have some lovely memories in *this* life and it's up to us to make that happen. Seems all he has brought with him so far have not been that pleasant and yes, I know he has told of us some good ones too, but we haven't dared ask him if he knows what this new life holds for him. He's told us about the rules in Heaven or the lessons they're supposed to have learnt before being accepted, but I still don't understand why he, or they, or everyone, has to come back to relearn stuff. We're mere mortals, Sarah. Your lad is the one who's teaching us. Life's too short to wait until a rainy day. So… you're OK with my suggestions, then?"

"One hundred percent. Oh, how exciting! I can't wait to go and have a look at some log cabins… Hang on a minute… you've already been looking, haven't you? I can tell!"

"Guilty," Bill laughed, "come, let me show you on the laptop. There are several for sale."

Bill went to his saved searches, showing Sarah the wonderful holiday homes in mid-Wales he'd favoured and on beautiful sites. "These are all three-bedroomed cabins and this one here, look, overlooks the lake and has a little decking area where we can sit outside and watch the ducks or the world go by whilst you and I have a little tipple on a warm evening. I've looked into everything, and we have to pay an annual ground rent for maintenance etc, and we can go practically anytime of the year, but I think I read where the site is closed for a month so that folk can't live there on a permanent basis."

"Perfect, Dad. Absolutely perfect. Good thinking, Batman. I cannot wait to go and have a proper look. What a pity you waited so long. Evan's at school; we could have spent months there. I remember Mum telling me how much she loved Wales when we used to go for our holidays, she said she felt she'd always come home."

"And maybe she did?" Bill added, "knowing what we know now, perhaps she did."

Sarah nodded, continuing to stare at the screen trying to imagine actually owning one of these idyllic constructions, "Perhaps, hey? And… thanks, Dad. Yes, let's do this. I'll let you tell Evan when I pick him up from school."

39: Tour de France, Partie Deux

Jack was taking some convincing whilst also seeing Eddie's logic. "And if everyone else has had the same thoughts?"

"Then we're finished and we go home, but at least we had a go. We're far from out of the woods yet. There's Volaart the Belgian veteran, this is his fourth... fifth time? This is our first attempt. Don't tell me you're prepared to drive us back to that wife of yours as a couple of failures?"

Jack succumbed to Eddie's thought pattern praying his assumptions were correct. They narrowly slid into position at the 10th after adhering to his suggestions and saved their stamina for the much-needed tortuous stages and beyond their wildest hopes and dreams, pedaled exhaustively to a fanfare of ecstatic well-wishers and supporters.

The two were spent, totally. They didn't think they could ever put their sore arses on another bike seat, let alone their legs work again. All they both wanted to do was sleep for a fortnight and have someone massage their weary and aching legs and shoulders.

"Remind me again, Kowalski, which idiot decided we undertake this stupid race?" Eddie asked while they lay side by side staring at the stars that flickered intermittently above that night, feeling the aches and pains in their bodies, both refusing to spend money on the offered accommodation. He received no answer because Jack was already snoring away like an old alcoholic.

Meanwhile, back in a little village on the outskirts of Dunkirk, Cindy opened her front door to the overwhelming welcome sight of her dear mother-in-law, Antonia, and she almost wept with joy upon seeing a familiar loving face.

Three weeks of being alone and having the horses, chickens, and everything else to see to made the arrival an absolute blessing. "I love my son, Cindy dearest, *ale to niedojrzały głupiec* (but he's an immature fool). Now, I'm here and praise the Lord for this wonderful weather. Let me see Armin after we've sat a while and chatted, I've missed the divine boy.

40: Eddie / Evan

Evan was sitting crossed legged on the living room floor surrounded by memoirs of his past life. Sarah debated leaving him alone to reflect as he'd requested, which saddened her a little because she felt she was being excluded.

"I haven't seen my family for a long time, Mum. I want to remember them all again and see how long they lived and where they lived afterwards. I want to see my other mum and dad, my sisters too. I haven't seen them in a long time," he said again.

Sarah stalled, not willing to leave him. "You mentioned some rules of being in Heaven, Evan. The rules or lessons, I can't remember... but do you remember what they are?"

He squinted as if trying to recall what he'd been told when he emerged from his own dark tunnel into the blinding bright glorious light and then was forced to watch his years on a huge display screen that hadn't yet been invented.

It had been an uncomfortable experience, more of an ordeal, as the kaleidoscope of memories flashed before him.

"I remember feeling so happy, exhausted but happy. Me and Jack were winners, Mum, we'd done it. But then I got this sudden pain for a split second and I didn't know why, why I felt distant… or why Jack's face was covered in blood. Jack wasn't smiling back at me and then I didn't see him after that."

Evan picked up several photographs and scrutinised each one.

"If you've been a murderer, before, then when you come back again you will be murdered. That's one of the lessons."

Sarah was mesmerised and hardly dared speak, "Go on."

"Everyone gets to see their mistakes. When I was Eddie I made many but I didn't know, then. Auntie Sylvia had to come back again because she experienced loss which wasn't her fault, but her parents blamed her. Not her mum and dad now, but her mum and dad before. You see, Mum, Auntie Sylvia was a man, before, and she insisted her brother Geordie, take part as a flag bearer. He was only 9 years old and now Auntie Sylvia has had to come back to acknowledge her lesson of guilt."

Sarah could almost understand that. "But you, Evan? Did you do something wrong, before? Is that why you're here again now, reborn to me?"

"No, Mum, not me," he answered most perfunctorily, "God sent me back to you so that *you* could learn *your* lesson."

Sarah had to leave him at that moment, feeling shaky and unworthy of being a parent. She was only going to be next door in the kitchen should he need a shoulder to cry on, but could never unhear his final words, "No, Mum, I was sent back again to *you* so that you could learn *your* lesson." What lesson? What had she done so wrong in her life that her own flesh and blood, her own damned child, was telling her she needed to learn a lesson?

It was inconceivable for her, as his mother, to consider her young son had not only been another person in a past life, a soldier who went to war, a dashing young man who won the Tour de France decades before she was even a glint in her father's eye… Yet Evan made it all sound so normal, but he'd returned to her so that she would have the opportunity to learn a lesson necessary for her to take back to the afterlife!

She was getting angrier and even more confused.

He'd described being in Heaven and meeting deceased family members, her very own unborn sister, her mother… She wondered if her mother had been afforded the same opportunity to be reborn and was there a child somewhere on the planet telling their mother of her own previous life? Would she ever know and would Evan eventually forget being Eddie Tyler and put the past behind him? According to everything she'd researched that's exactly what did happen and so she concluded it had been very necessary to allow him to express himself and talk about it whenever he wanted to.

She was immensely grateful to Edward Tyler, this Great-great-uncle of hers for coming back to her as her divine and wonderful son and she would continue to honour his memory of everything they'd found in the little cream vanity case her mother had kept, vowing it would never leave their sight, hidden away up in the attic again, but also felt extremely angry at being informed he'd been born to teach her a lesson!

It may well be that Evan will forget. Time will tell, but Sarah would never. When he was ready, she would take him to the cemetery and lay some flowers on his grave, perhaps that would bring closure? She needed to tie up some loose ends first, though.

One, she needed to ascertain how he died, because according to Evan, he died in France but it must have been after the war because he'd returned to take part in the cycling tournament with Jack in France, and Evan had declared that's where he'd died! How had he died?

Two, assuming his body had been returned to England, why was he not buried in any of the Ibstock cemeteries where all his family lived?

The kitchen door was slightly ajar and Sarah could hear muffled chattering coming from the living room. Evan was talking to the photographs, and although she didn't really want to be eavesdropping it was human-nature or motherly nosiness to strain her ears to listen…

"I'm sorry everyone for all the sadness I caused. I'm sorry, Mum, that you had to lose both sons. I'm sorry I wasn't at your wedding, May, but you told me you'd been happy with Will. And Meg… I came to see you straight away to say sorry to you, first. I wanted to be Bert's best man, but I had to go, you see. I couldn't help it. It was part of the rules."

Tears ran down Sarah's cheeks. He was apologising to his family for dying! It was utterly heartbreaking and she was annoyed at herself for not having all the details at her disposal to give the child everything he needed to process!

She went back to her laptop, opened it up and typed in Edward Tyler, Tour de France, after WW I, livid with herself for not thinking about that earlier.

And there it was…

A list of all the one hundred and thirty-eight competitors and the countries they were representing. Photographs of the start, photographs along the course, the whole race, and the finishing line. The same photograph she'd found before with Eddie and Jack, Eddie's arms around the shoulders of his smaller-framed friend, a whole running commentary of the three weeks' prestigious event, and then she gasped in horror, covering her mouth as she continued scrolling down, stalling as the bold headlines of the French newspaper appeared…

"Tragedy at Tour de France Celebrations"

*   *   *   *   *

Bill and Sarah leaned close together while they watched Evan lay a circular wreath of laurel leaves and arum lilies on top of Edward Tyler's grave, befitting a cycling champion, they decided, after leaving a bunch of daffodils and tulips on Pat's.

Edward Tyler's tombstone was small, insignificant, covered in lichen and the inscription now barely legible. There was a fresh spray of mimosa laying there, which surprised the two adults, and when Evan lay down his floral tribute he picked up the mimosa and inhaled its weak perfume.

"From my dad's shop," he announced, looking around as if he anticipated seeing someone who'd been there.

Smiling reassuringly, he turned to face his grandfather and mother. "We can go home now, Mum. It's OK, it's all finished. Shall we go home?"

So they did.

41: *Le Miroir de Paris, 1920*

'*Tragédie lors des célébrations du Tour de France*'
(Tragedy at Tour de France Celebrations)

One British competitor was shot dead and another seriously wounded at the climax of this year's Tour de France, in Paris last night amid tumultuous celebrations.

The Englishman has been named as WW I veteran of the DSO Edward Tyler from Leicestershire in England. Tyler was announced overall winner of the event with his comrade, Jack Kowalski (owner of the Kowalski Equestrian Centre in Dunkirk, also a WW I veteran) - who is undergoing treatment for a gunshot wound to his shoulder - as runner up. Tyler was pronounced dead upon arrival at the newly built hospital in Boucicaut where Kowalski remains in a stable condition.

Horrified onlookers forcibly restrained elderly Pascal Enrique who, when questioned about his motives, simply stated, "They left us to starve to death." At this stage, the meaning of his declaration is unclear, but he is currently being detained in a psychiatric unit awaiting further assessment.

Five weeks later, a forlorn and subdued Jack Kowalski returned to his idyllic cottage on the outskirts of Dunkirk where he was reunited with Armin, his beautiful wife, his adored mother, and his new baby daughter.

He took a sledgehammer to his pushbike the morning after he returned home, saddled up Armin, and galloped into the hillside to watch the sunset where he sat and sobbed.

42: Postscript and Author Notes

This novel, 'Before I Was Me', is based upon my own personal interest and research into children who openly talk about their past lives. A subject debatable but can't be dismissed glibly. My own nephew talked about being 'before he was a baby in his mother's tummy' and scientific statements that left us gobsmacked. The children that have these so-called recollections are usually advanced in their development. The big words, constructed sentences, empathy and an overall appearance of being an old soul in a child's body.

Will we ever know? Perhaps, one day, or maybe not ever.

My dear grandma, Meg Knifton (nee Tyler) was considered (nowadays) as 'Fey' (visionary; otherworldly) though at the time she was always poo-pooed by her family and in fact it was her brother Johnny who was the cyclist and not Eddie; I altered the names purely for the book. Johnny did die after winning a cycling tournament, in Hugglescote, at the corner of Manor Road / Richmond Road. My grandmother was scrubbing the backyard step when she felt a presence next to her asking what she would wear, and she replied, "my mothers's black coat, of course." When her mother asked who she was taking to she replied, "Nobody," because there wasn't anyone there - yet my grandmother told me there was: her brother Johnny - she felt - had to come to make amends as they'd argued before he went off to the race.

(Incidentally, according to the Family Tree we have had done, Johnny Tyler Junior was also in the Coldstream Guards, and it was HE in fact who was discharged due to ill health and not his father.)

Likewise, my great-grandparents did marry at the chapel at The Tower of London by special permission of Queen Victoria when he was 19 and she was 21, where my Great-grandfather - John Tyler - stood sentry outside Her Majesty's bedroom (we have the banns and wedding certification as proof). My Great-grandfather's portrait - allegedly to this day - still hangs in the Horseguards Officers' Mess (according to our cousin Kevin Atkins who was also in the Coldstream Guards). My Great-grandmother was a descendant of the Huguenots that came to England during the mass exodus of the Huguenots during the French Revolution. My 93 year-old mother recalls receiving parcels from France, as a child, including silk socks for her and her sister and a little naval uniform for her brother, from relatives still residing in France. We have a Maynard Crest of Arms too.

Albert Knifton - Bert - my maternal grandfather was indeed a crack shot sniper during the First World War who absolutely did go AWOL, his desertion a result of a breakdown and walked from London to Leicestershire whilst on leave in an effort to end his years of misery. The firing squad, I imagine, was a far more welcome vision to consider facing rather than having to endure unknown more years being ordered to kill, again and again and again, but his expertise as a gunman prevented that. My grandad was a very quiet unassuming man who offered little to conversations when we visited other than to ask us to sit on his knee and comb his thinning white hair whilst he would stare blankly into the flames of the coal fire, rubbing his hands together, constantly.

My mother clearly recalls one Christmas dinner with the family sat around the dining table as her dad stood to carve the chicken. Chicken was a luxury back then and it was one of their own reared which my grandmother had had to kill because my grandfather declared his killing days were over! And as my mother's father poised to carve the bird, he faltered... mumbling "It was either him or me." Nobody deemed to ask him what he meant. It was Christmas Day! What memories he was recalling were never known because nobody asked the questions as everyone wiped away their tears. Was he remembering the Christmas Day Truce? Possibly. He returned from the war a damaged man - along with many others.

As twenty-first century people we are lucky to have the internet at our disposal to research our past, as I've tried to portray with Sarah and Bill listening to Evan and their willingness to learn and help him transgress safely and securely from the past to his present. If my own grandfather had been shown just an ounce of the same compassion, he probably wouldn't have had such a lonely life which he declared was "all bed and work," and is something again my mother still berates herself over for being too young to understand.

Yet it is all history: no clocks can be turned back, no chance of second chances, and all beyond our reparation. It took me only 16 days to write this novel as I couldn't stop tapping away at the keyboard. I just hope I've managed to make my family happy to bring some of our ancestors/relatives to life once more. Not just for us but also for my friend, Chris Kowalski, who honored me to pass on some of his own personal family history, enabling this novel another dimension. Chris has a whole magnificent catalogue of memoirs for his own book waiting to be written.

"*Mais d'ici là, puissions-nous tous vivre heureux et en bonne santé.*"

(But until then, may we all live happily and in good health.)

XXX

Acknowledgements

As always, I give my most sincere thanks to my lovely ladies who give up their valuable time to read and send me a list of my many errors. They are: first off my 93 year-old mother who reads the lot, then Susan Bond, Sue Robins, and a dear old friend, Karen Aldridge

I have to acknowledge Chris Kowalski again for allowing me to use his own family history in this novel.

Cover image, courtesy of philnicholson.photography. Thank you, Phil, for your patience and interpreting my vision. I love it!

Finally, my sincerest of thanks and appreciation I bestow to Michael Paul Hurd of Lineage Independent Publishing who is the sole reason for this, my seventh novel, to reach my readers. Without him, my scribbles would remain pushed inside a cupboard.

Reincarnation isn't everyone's belief, I acknowledge that and my books are all fictional whilst at the same time include many facts, both historical and personal memories.

Thank you for reading.

Lisa Talbott, Summer of 2024

Printed in Great Britain
by Amazon

46368795R00179